CALL TO GLORY

He was descended from a long line of fighters. Now Lieutenant Coy Vestal must leave Fort Bragg and take on a real challenge that would test the family tradition of pride and courage . . .

After waiting five long months in the desert, the 82nd Airborne Division, known as the All-Americans, springs into action against a Republican Guard armored battalion. Vestal's antitank company, fighting alongside the Scouts, must ambush armor units with a full arsenal of TOW missile launchers, AT-4 recoilless launchers, and MK-19 automatic grenade launchers.

The enemy is relentless. The sandstorms are worse. But no one ever said war was easy . . .

AIRBORNE

Book One of the Explosive New Saga by L. T. Hagan

BOOK ONE

AIRBORNE

CALL TO GLORY

L. T. Hagan

BERKLEY BOOKS, NEW YORK

AIRBORNE: CALL TO GLORY

A Berkley Book / published by arrangement with
the author

PRINTING HISTORY
Berkley edition / January 1993

ISBN: 0-425-13575-6

A BERKLEY BOOK ® TM 757,375
Berkley Books are published by The Berkley Publishing Group,
200 Madison Avenue, New York, New York 10016.
The name "BERKLEY" and the "B" logo
are trademarks belonging to Berkley Publishing Corporation.

PRINTED IN THE UNITED STATES OF AMERICA

10 9 8 7 6 5 4 3 2 1

This book is dedicated to the warriors of Desert Storm—the men and women who stood defiantly in the sand and brought home the glory. A special dedication to the elite, the 82nd Airborne Division, America's Guard of Honor, for portraying, as they always do, the very best in America.

Special thanks to Ron, Deidre, Win, Molly, Scott and Maggie for their undeniable assistance and endless patience

"There are three kinds of men:
The living, the dead, and the Airborne!"

—Gen. Carl W. Stiner
USSOCOM CINC

CALL TO GLORY

Cadet Coy Vestal leaned against the wall and stared out the window of his room. From the fourth floor, he had a clear view of the Hudson River, dark and swift from the spring rains, as it surged past its verdant banks. Unusually warm weather had forced the trees to bud and bloom ahead of time, producing a profusion of color on the normally drab landscape.

Vestal watched as the graduating cadets' relatives mixed with alumni and visiting dignitaries on their way to the reviewing stands.

He had less than an hour before he would join the formation and graduate from West Point, less than an hour before he would be a brand new second lieutenant, the first in his military family to graduate from the Academy, the first to be a commissioned officer.

His roommate was already out there with the other graduates. They were all looking forward to what would be one of the happiest days of their lives, a moment of achievement, the great beginning for which they had labored. Vestal stared out the window, waiting for some feeling of euphoria to sweep over him.

1

He didn't feel the joy, the excitement, the sense of achievement. He was feeling his stomach tighten from the slow constriction of his own internal pressures.

Turning from the window, he glanced across the room at the packed boxes and footlockers awaiting shipment. Everything he owned was in these boxes, neatly packed. All his uniforms, boots, books— everything he looked to for answers was contained in the crates. He realized, as he looked over it all, how very little there was. Like the packed belongings, he was now an alien in the stark little room. He could no longer find refuge here; like these boxes, he was awaiting transport to a new location.

No doubt the uniforms, all expensively tailored and made of the finest materials, would be perfect for their call to duty, but, Vestal thought as his stomach knotted, was he?

Would the uniforms, so perfect in every detail, cover up the man inside, the man who desperately wished he wasn't leaving West Point, the man who would now be called on to perform?

He absentmindedly straightened his tunic, running his fingers over the woolen fabric. These were the last moments of privacy for the day; shortly he would become one more in a "long gray line," one more piece of the great tradition of the United States Military Academy.

As he nervously clenched and unclenched his fist, he studied the class ring on his finger. It seemed heavy, a colossal weight, as if it contained all the responsibilities and duties expected of him.

He wished his father were there. He needed a chance to talk to him, to ask him if he had ever been afraid, if he had ever felt unsure, if he had ever felt confusion. But those were questions that could never be answered. His father was long gone, a hero, fallen on the field of honor in Southeast Asia. His death and posthumous Medal of Honor had been Vestal's ticket to West Point.

Perhaps his uncles, all Airborne, all retired now as sergeants major, could answer those questions, but Vestal knew he wouldn't ask them. They were out there now with his mother, waiting anxiously to see him graduate.

He couldn't possibly admit fear, confusion, his unsure concept of himself to them. He was John Vestal's only child, his son, and the last fragment they had of their heroic brother. He couldn't let them know how he was feeling now. He didn't have the right to spoil their illusion of who he was. And right now, that was all he really was—an illusion of a strong military man, a new officer, a man who knew where he was going, what he was made of, and who would lead men into battle. He shook in his shoes, looking back out the window as the door swung open.

"Hey, Coy! Your uncles are downstairs waiting. They want to walk over to formation with you."

Vestal, yanked abruptly from his thoughts, turned to face Vince Caruso. His roommate was flushed with excitement as he stood nervously in the door.

"I'm on my way down. You ready for your big 'moment of truth'?" Vestal said, forcing a smile.

3

"That's affirmative! I am ready to shed this place and get on with it," Caruso answered, looking at his watch. "We better get a move on."

"Hey," Vestal reached over to pick up his hat, "I wasn't talking about graduation. You're getting married tomorrow, remember? That's the 'moment of truth,' when your beautiful fiancée finds out how bad your breath is in the morning!"

"Man," Caruso strutted in the doorway, smoothing his tunic, "she's so dazzled by my manliness, she'll never notice. I gotta go, she's waiting for me. Don't forget to bring your mother to the rehearsal dinner tonight."

Vestal nodded and waved as his roommate charged off down the hall. He walked into the hallway, took one last glance into the room, then closed the door behind him. It was time for the "illusion" to perform, time to close all doors behind him and face whatever stood before him.

George Patton "Jeep" Laliker waited in front of the building, feeling as conspicuous and uncomfortable as the bastard child at a family reunion.

One thing was for sure, his Texas A&M uniform—the traditional Eisenhower jacket, with the Sam Browne belt over the gray-pink jodhpurs and highly polished brown riding boots—stood out. He reached up and adjusted his campaign hat, worn with this uniform only on auspicious occasions, and tried to ignore the stares of the people passing by.

Glancing down at his watch for the fifth time in

fifteen minutes, Jeep sighed and shifted nervously from one foot to the other.

The two stars on his shoulder designated his position in the Corps at A&M, Cadet Lieutenant Colonel, the highest rank possible, first in his graduating class. That position had earned him a Regular Army commission upon graduation, in a day when many of the graduates were being released to the reserves to serve their commitments. Jeep was proud of his position, proud of his high standing at A&M, but here at West Point, alma mater of past generations of the Laliker family, he was experiencing a recurring sense of failure.

This was where he had thought he would be. He had dreamed and planned since he was a child of standing here today, waiting to graduate from the Academy. He had done everything necessary to become accepted—the high grade average, the leadership positions in high school programs, participation in sports. West Point looked for the complete individual, well rounded and excelling in all areas. Jeep was a contender.

The sports had been his downfall. To become captain of his high school football team, he had taken one too many chances on the field, played with everything in him, and broken his leg in the last season. The break and subsequent lengthy healing period had cost him his slot as first alternate to the U.S. Military Academy. It had been a bitter disappointment, one that rose up in his mind and haunted him still.

Even though his family had played down his loss,

encouraging him to take the scholarship to Texas A&M, he knew he was the only male member of his family, since the establishment of the Military Academy, to not attend. Admitting defeat was also not a family trait, and Jeep had hidden his disappointment, working hard to recover from the broken leg and pushing himself to the limit at A&M. He never discussed his missed opportunity at the Academy and overachieved to fill his personal void.

His father had graduated high in his class, gone into the infantry, earned his Airborne wings and served two tours in Vietnam with the 101st. On his second tour his APC had hit a land mine and he'd lost one arm and both legs. Even though he had retired from the military on a medical discharge, he kept close contact with his fellow graduates, never missing a graduation.

In years past, Mrs. Laliker had attended the ceremonies with her husband, helping him maneuver around the campus in his wheelchair, but this year Jeep's grandmother had been hospitalized the week before graduation, forcing his mother to stay behind. When she called and asked Jeep to attend, she hadn't realized the effect it would have on her son.

So here he stood, anguishing instead of celebrating. This was Senior Week back at College Station. There, he'd be going out to parties, accepting all the honor and respect he'd gained as Cadet Lieutenant Colonel. Instead, he was standing on the campus of the school he hadn't measured up to, waiting to watch graduate the men and women who would always have date-of-rank on him by one week, while his father visited with old friends in the building behind him.

To pass the time, he watched the passersby as they congregated in little groups around the walkway, waiting for the graduation parade to start. He glanced down at his watch again and was pleased to see it was nearing time for him to go back inside for his father. He turned and walked past three sergeants major standing in their uniforms by the door. He bounded up the stairs, swung open the door and collided with a cadet in the doorway, knocking the man off balance. The cadet's hat fell and rolled out on the step.

"Whoa!" Laliker said, stepping back to steady himself.

"Hey!" the startled cadet yelled, watching as the man in front of him backed up. "Watch it! You're standing on my hat!"

Laliker looked down. Sure enough, he had planted one of his boots squarely on the brim of the cadet's hat. As he reached down to retrieve it, they bumped heads, knocking Laliker back a step. Before Jeep could apologize, the angry cadet yanked the hat from the ground, muttering under his breath, and took a long look at the offender.

As he nervously wiped at the scrape on the highly polished brim, he looked up at Laliker.

"You clumsy bastard!" A twisted smile formed on his lips as he recognized the A&M uniform. "What are you dressed up for?" he asked. "A costume ball?

Looks like you wore the wrong costume for this party, 'Second-stringer.'"

Laliker, incensed by the insult, squared his jaw and stepped forward. "Look, you arrogant asshole, I—"

"Gentlemen!" A voice barked out from behind them.

They both turned to see who was speaking. A gray-haired major, who bore a striking resemblance to the A&M cadet, scowled at them both from his wheelchair. The West Point cadet came to attention and saluted as Laliker stepped past him and stood behind the chair.

"Sir," the cadet stammered, pushing the door open, "allow me."

Major Laliker returned the salute and nodded as Jeep, eyes blazing, pushed the wheelchair past and down the ramp.

The cadet hurriedly joined some older men and rushed past the Lalikers to the formation. Jeep watched, still stinging from his slur, as he pushed his father toward the reviewing stands in silence. After the chair had been placed on the stand, Jeep walked around and stood beside his dad.

Major Laliker had been glancing through the program, giving his son time to cool down. He cleared his throat. "You want to talk about that?" he said, looking up at Jeep.

"No, I expected it!" Jeep said angrily.

The major shifted uncomfortably in the chair. "Get the chip off your shoulder, son. It doesn't become you. He didn't mean what he said."

8

"The hell he didn't!"

"Look," Major Laliker said, as the band struck the first chords of a march and the parade began, "he's strung tight today; so are you. Just write it off to nerves. I saw his name tag and looked him up. That's John Vestal's son. He's probably a good man."

"Vestal?" Jeep questioned, looking down at his father. "He graduated with you?"

"No, John Vestal was a master sergeant and died in Vietnam. He was awarded the Medal of Honor."

"Just because his dad died to get him into the Academy, doesn't mean he's a 'good man.'"

"Well, you could be right. At any rate, you'll have the opportunity to find out soon enough. You're both headed in the same direction," Major Laliker said, looking out over the cadets as they marched by. "The program has the destination of each cadet next to his name. Just like you, Coy Vestal is headed for Ranger school and the 82nd Airborne Division."

CHAPTER ONE

"Platoons form up!"

It was six o'clock in the morning, but a hot August sun was already on the rise as the first sergeant of D Company, 1st of the 325th, called out to the assembled men.

The sound of "Jody calls" thundered through the headquarters area as the 82nd Airborne Division began its daily physical training exercise, or "PT" as it was fondly referred to by the soldiers.

"Where's the El-T?" whispered Sergeant Harold McIver to Sergeant First Class Van Hallmark, standing next to him.

"On the way. Get in formation, McIver," Hallmark said, his eyes searching the parking lot for Lieutenant Coy Vestal's red pickup truck. "Let the officers be worrying about the officers and we NCOs will handle business."

"I hate this shit!" mumbled Corporal Eustas Lee Sommerhill.

"Stop sniveling, Sommerhill." Hallmark's eyes swept the horizon again as he formed up his platoon. "The Airborne don't snivel. We all hate this shit."

As he was speaking, Vestal's '57 Ford slammed to a stop in the lot across from them. The lieutenant emerged, left the door standing open and broke into a dead sprint to join the already moving formation.

"Mornin', El-T." Hallmark greeted him. "Perfect timing."

Vestal adjusted his pace and fell into the "Airborne shuffle" as the company headed down Ardennes Street. "Might have been a little too close this morning, Hallmark. I have the attention of Captain Rodwell." He nodded to the man standing on the curb with his hands on his hips.

"Save your breath for the run, Lieutenant!" Rodwell barked and fell in next to Vestal. "Perhaps we've scheduled PT too early for you. Shall I speak to General Johnson and have the Division reschedule?"

"No, sir! Failure to maintain vehicle repair, sir. Won't happen again!" Vestal panted out.

"Damn right it won't!" Rodwell growled as he sprinted forward to take his place at the head of D Company.

"Vehicle?! You mean *wreck*! What's the prob, Vestal? Sleep late?" a voice called out from behind, well within Rodwell's hearing.

Vestal snapped around to see Jeep Laliker jogging behind him. "Thanks for your concern."

Laliker smiled from ear to ear as he watched Rodwell look back at Vestal again.

"Lieutenant Vestal! Eyes forward and run. This isn't social hour," Rodwell asked. "Be in my office at fourteen hundred hours and don't be late."

"Yes, sir," Vestal answered. He could hear Jeep laughing all the way down Ardennes.

The back of his BDUs were smoking and shredded after Rodwell's ass-chewing that afternoon. Surviving that, he'd spent the last four hours working on the truck over at the 82nd auto shop. The surly relic still belched smoke and misfired as he came around the statue of "Iron Mike" and pulled into the parking lot at the club. He was frustrated and tired.

It was Friday night, and the crowd at Willy's, the bar in the basement of the officers' club, was bigger and wilder than usual. It had taken a supreme effort to shower and dress to get there. Vestal wasn't sure why he was subjecting himself to the "press of flesh."

He spotted an empty slot down near the pro shop and was about to pull in when a silver Mazda shot past him and into it, causing him to slam on his brakes to avoid a collision.

"Hey!" Vestal leaned out the window as the Mazda door opened. "Don't you—" He stopped abruptly as a pair of bare, long legs slid out of the driver's side. He swallowed hard as the legs stood. She was a dynamite redhead in the shortest, tightest minidress he'd ever seen. It was at that moment that he remembered why he was going to Willy's.

"I'm sorry, I didn't realize you were going to park here. I thought you were the maintenance man for the golf club." She smiled as she looked over the

12

smoking old pickup, and Vestal found himself smiling back.

"Are you making fun of my truck?"

She laughed and started toward the entrance. He spotted a place farther off and pulled in. He didn't have to turn off the engine; it died as he stopped. He wiggled the key in the ignition. Nothing, no spark of life.

He looked back to see if the girl was still there. "Shit!" Vestal hit the wheel with his fist as he saw Jeep Laliker walking with her into the club.

Willy's crowd was young. This was where the lieutenants and captains partied . . . and where all the best-looking women in the Fayetteville area converged on Friday nights. There was plenty of action, but the image of the redhead was etched on his brain as Coy Vestal looked around the bar.

Yep, Laliker was definitely putting the moves on her. Vestal watched as Jeep ordered drinks then turned to give her the full impact of his profile.

Coy stood behind two tall lieutenants and called down the bar. "Hey, Jeep! You left your lights on." He ducked down between the two and shielded his face.

Laliker turned to see who had called out as the mane of strawberry curls bobbed, repeating the message to him. He threw up his hands in apology, then left by the side door.

Vestal moved in. "Let's dance," he said, grabbing her hand as he walked quickly toward the dance floor. She offered a token resistance, then followed

13

him. They found a spot and he pulled her close to him.

"Hi!" he said, looking down into wide green eyes in a field of freckles. "Sorry I'm late. Someone got my parking place."

She laughed, displaying a dazzlingly white smile. "I didn't know I was waiting for you . . . Who are you, anyway?"

"Coy, Coy Vestal, maintenance man. And you?"

She laughed again and he liked the sound of it. "Colleen Harrigan. I'm sorry about the parking place. I've seen that ol— that truck before. Aren't you with the Division?"

"Uh-huh. You work on post, Colleen?"

"Call me Colley. I'm an MP with the Division. You know you have a cracked taillight, don't you?"

"The least of my problems. It's hard to get parts for that thing. Are you going to arrest me?"

"Maybe I should . . . Why, do you want me to?"

She was flirting. It was the first sign Vestal's luck was changing. "I don't know," he said, pulling her tighter, "the idea of you and a set of handcuffs is exciting."

Jeep Laliker pushed his way across the room toward them. "Cheap trick, Vestal! They teach you that at the 'high-school on the Hudson'?" He barreled up to them on the dance floor.

"Come on, Colley," he said as he reached for her hand, "let's get out of here."

"Easy, Jeep! She's improved her status and is with me!" Vestal turned his back and continued dancing Colley toward the center of the floor.

Jeep's hand shot out and grabbed Vestal's shoulder, yanking Coy backward.

"Hands off, Bud!" Vestal said, releasing his grip on Colley and turning toward Jeep.

"Oh, shit! Why don't you two just dance with each other!" Colleen said and walked off the floor, leaving the two lieutenants glaring at each other. She grabbed her purse from the bar and hurried out the door.

"Great," Jeep said, watching her leave, "now she's gone. I oughta clean your clock, you asshole!" He pushed Vestal backward.

"I told you to keep your hands off," Vestal pushed back.

A crowd formed around the two on the dance floor. Catcalls from the onlookers urged them on. Both men were squared off and facing each other with clenched fists. They didn't need much encouragement.

"You want to fight, take it to the gym!" The voice booming out was that of Captain Rodwell as he shoved his way through the throng to the two lieutenants.

"Fine with me, sir," Vestal said, his jaw muscles clenching as he glared at Jeep.

"See you at Callahan's Gym, in the ring, tomorrow morning," Jeep responded.

"OK," Rodwell looked with disdain at them both, "Zero nine-thirty tomorrow morning. Now, you idiots, get the hell out of here before your girlfriend comes back with a squad of MPs." He pushed them both toward the door. "That's all I need, a blotter

15

entry for officers brawling publicly in the club. I'm warning you, Airborne, you better *never* embarrass me!"

Jeep jumped into his GEO Storm and passed dangerously close to Vestal on his way out of the parking lot. Vestal dodged the car and opened the door to his truck. He jammed the key into the ignition, then remembered, as nothing happened, that the truck had died earlier. "Damn!"

News of the match spread rapidly during the night, and a mob had already formed as the two combatants arrived. Members of D Company filled the gym on Reilly Road and boisterously made bets on their favorite.

Rodwell stood at the door, dressed in his gray running shorts and D Company T-shirt. He scowled across the room as Laliker and Vestal, standing in the ring in their sparring equipment, listened to the referee explain the rules of the fight.

"OK," explained the ref, "you know the drill. No holding, no hitting below the belt, first blood drawn ends the fight. Now, shake hands and may the best man win."

Laliker and Vestal touched gloves and went to their corners. SFC. Hallmark met Vestal and shoved the protective mouthpiece between his lips. "I guess there's no way out of this," he said as he checked the lacing on Vestal's glove. "You know this is stupid."

"Yeah, but inevitable. Laliker's been on my back

since Ranger school," Vestal mumbled, while Hall-mark tightened and straightened his gear.

The bell rang, and each man aggressively rushed to meet the other in the center of the ring. Laliker delivered the first punch, a quick right hook that barely touched Vestal's jaw. Coy was fast with a return, throwing a hard left to Jeep's temple.

Laliker staggered back but recovered and jabbed with his right again, this time connecting dead center in the middle of Vestal's face. Vestal fell back, almost going to his knees. Jeep slid forward rapidly, moving on his advantage to deliver the knockout punch as Vestal yanked back up and sidestepped him.

Sneakers scuffed over the canvas as they danced around each other, neither able to find an opening. The bell rang, and as each returned to his own area for a gulp of water, the ref dashed between them, checking for blood. Finding none on either fighter, he signaled the timekeeper that the fight was still on.

The bell rang signaling the second round as D Company's Officer of the Day came through the door and hurried over to Captain Rodwell. The two men moved out of hearing range and carried on a hurried exchange as Vestal and Laliker scurried out to face each other in the ring.

Vestal pulled a left hook and connected, slam-ming Laliker into the ropes hard. The crowd roared, voicing an even mixture of encouragement for Vestal and Laliker. The bell rang again, sending Vestal to his corner as the ref rushed to Laliker and checked him. Laliker clung to the ropes, down on one knee, but as the bell sounded, he yanked himself to his feet and pushed away from the side of the ring.

"No blood, no blood, keep the fight going," he mumbled to the ref as the official checked his face. A large blue-purple bruise throbbed painfully over his left eye, but there was no blood. The ref signaled and the bell sounded again.

Vestal had barely stepped out of his corner when Laliker charged him, slamming a left-right combination to his face, knocking out his mouthpiece. Vestal dropped to both knees but rolled out and sprang back to his feet. He caught Laliker around the waist. Both fighters clung to each other as the ref blew his whistle. Before releasing his hold, Coy whispered into Laliker's ear, "Now you've done it, you bastard!"

The ref pushed them apart, sending each man to his corner. Hallmark shoved the mouthpiece back into Vestal's mouth. "It's a tie, sir. Quit, now."

"No way," Vestal muttered through the mouthpiece. His face, though uncut, was showing effects of the beating. His upper lip was swollen twice its normal size. The slightest tap would make it burst, delivering the blood needed to end the fight, and Jeep would be well aware of this vulnerable spot once Vestal turned around.

"Stop the fight!" Rodwell shouted, moving away from the duty officer. He grabbed the ropes and swung up into the ring. "All members of the 82nd are to report to their units immediately. Repeat, all members of the 82nd are to report to their units immediately." Loud groans issued up from the crowd as the gym emptied.

"You two," Rodwell grabbed Vestal and Laliker by their gloves, "declare a truce and get to the Company. It's a move-out. Get going!" He released them and jumped out of the ring. They watched as he walked briskly out the door.

Laliker turned to look at Vestal. "Almost had you, didn't I?"

"How can you tell, I mean . . . can you really see out of that eye?" Coy slurred through his swollen lip.

"It's over. Both of you heroes beat the shit out of each other. Now, let's get out of here." Hallmark stepped between them and pushed Vestal toward the ropes.

Jeep dropped his sparing gear on the desk as he went out the front door. Hallmark placed Vestal's gloves and helmet into a basket by the ring. "My ride left me. I'll hitch one with you to the Company, if that's OK, El-T."

"Sure. You think this deal is over Hussein's invasion of Kuwait?" Vestal wiped his face and tossed the towel on the desk as they moved toward the door.

"No doubt about it. I hear Saudi Arabia is hotter than hell this time of year!" Hallmark picked up his gym bag and fell in behind him.

As they walked out into the sunshine, they saw an MP stuffing a piece of paper under Vestal's windshield wiper. Coy recognized the well-formed shape of Colleen Harrigan as she slid back into the patrol car.

"Looks like you got a ticket, El-T!" Hallmark said, watching the MP car pull out onto Reilly Road.

"Maybe not," Vestal said, as Colley waved back at him. "I think she likes me."

"I've seen her with Laliker at the club over in the Holiday Inn. They looked like they might be dancin' in a room there, not just dancin' in the club, if you catch my drift."

"Naw, probably wasn't her, but even if it was she moved up in the world last night." He smiled broadly at Hallmark and pulled two scraps of paper from under the wiper.

"Well?" Hallmark watched as Vestal's smile faded.

"Mixed message . . . Seems I've been cited for a cracked taillight, officially, but the unofficial note says 'See you in Saudi.'"

CHAPTER TWO

"This is bullshit! I don't want to go fight my Muslim brothers." Corporal Sommerhill was an unhappy man as he loaded on to the waiting C-141.

"Sommerhill, quit your bitching! You aren't Muslim, your dog tag says you're Catholic." Hallmark was behind him as they entered the aircraft.

"Well, I been meaning to change that, Sarge. My wife Kisha says this is against our Muslim brothers over oil. I don't own a gas station either!"

"She said that, did she?" Hallmark grimaced. "Well, I imagine she's going to need some oil to propel that hot little Miata around North Carolina while you're gone."

"That's another thing, Sarge. I mean, I need to see the chaplin. Kisha and I have been having some marital disputes lately. This just isn't a good time for me to be leaving."

"What you call a *marital dispute* has resulted in seven MP calls for domestic disturbances." Hallmark laughed as he sat down and adjusted his gear. "Hell, son, we may save your life by taking you to war."

Sommerhill smiled sheepishly. "Well, she does have a prickly disposition . . . but it's because she's just not adjusted to her new environment. She says Ft. Bragg is dangerous."

Hallmark stared at him. "Are you shittin' me? You told me she came from Detroit, from a crack ghetto, where crime has skyrocketed. Hell, this is the first time she's ever seen someone run down the street for exercise. Where she came from, they were running for their lives."

"I know . . . but, well, she says it's a racist place. She says they're using the brothers again to fight a white man's war."

Hallmark sighed. "Sommerhill, look at me."

"Yes, Sarge."

"What color am I?"

"Why you're white, but—"

"No," Hallmark interrupted. "Listen, are we related?"

"Well, no, Sarge, but . . ."

"Damned right," he interrupted again as he leaned over and grabbed Sommerhill's sleeve. "But you see, Corporal," he said, roughly tapping the Division patch, "we wear the same suit and the same patch; we're on the same damned airplane, going the same damned place . . . so you can tell Kisha to stop with the old boonie rap about fighting for white men. That was yesterday's news."

Sommerhill squirmed on the bench as Hallmark released his sleeve. He watched the sergeant lean back, fold his arms over his reserve chute and close his eyes. "You goin' to sleep, Sarge?"

Hallmark opened one eye. "Do I have a choice or

have you got some other load of shit you need to discuss, son?"

The corporal took a deep breath. "Sarge, I think I should tell you. I don't like jumping out of airplanes."

"Extra bucks, Sommerhill, and the privilege of an Airborne funeral. That's why we all do it. Now, I want you to give it a rest and stop sniveling. You'll need strength in a few hours to fight Muslims . . . You see, they don't know they're your brothers."

Sommerhill's eyes widened. It was obvious that he hadn't really given that any thought. He looked around at the others in the dim glow of the red lights inside the aircraft. Some were sleeping, or at least appeared to be sleeping. He decided that although he wasn't feeling that cool, he could at least appear to be. He leaned back, closed his eyes and pondered how to convince those Arabs that he was one of them. He wished he could at least speak their language.

SFC. Hallmark remained still until he heard Sommerhill snoring, then moved down the bench to a vacant spot by Harold McIver. Somehow Mac had smuggled his laptop computer on board and was busily blasting his way through a video game.

McIver, Hallmark decided, was the consummate nerd. Sitting inside a dimly lit C-141 on a trip to god-knows-where, McIver had taped a small Maglite to his glasses so he could see.

"How's it going, McIver?" Hallmark said as he scrunched in beside him.

"Huh!" McIver yanked himself out of his video

trance and swung his head around toward Hallmark, bouncing the beam of the Mag-lite around
the interior. "Oh, fine, Sarge," he said, looking
straight at Hallmark. The high intensity beam of
the little flashlight hit Hallmark directly in the
eyes.

Hallmark raised his hand and gently turned off
the Mag-lite. "Good. That's good. You got a real
challenge here with the Mario Brothers?" he asked,
referring to the famous video game.

McIver's eyes, magnified by his thick glasses,
blinked. "Really, Sarge, that's for children. No, I've
got my own game programmed in here." His pupils
dilated with excitement as he reached up and
flipped on his Mag-lite. "See," he said, swinging his
head down to focus on the game board in his hands,
"it's a simulated tank battle, using TOWs and
grenade launchers against Russian tanks."

His hands moved like lightning across the con-
trols, and the screen lit up, displaying a myriad of
what looked like dots and dashes to Hallmark.
McIver, thrilled to have Hallmark's interest, excitedly began to explain the game.

"You have a limit on ammo and positions as the
tanks move forward. They, of course, have their
own limitations on mobility, but the advantage of
being able to deliver awesome firepower. The edge,
I'm sure you see," he said, adjusting his glasses, "is
the mobility of the TOW crews."

Hallmark was, by his own admission, totally
computer illiterate . . . and liked it that way.

"Uh-huh," he said, staring at McIver's toy. "You designed and programmed this game yourself?"

McIver, mistaking Hallmark's disinterest for criticism, deflated. His skinny shoulders slumped forward. "Well, Sarge, I didn't have time to get some of my more complicated games installed. I know this one is rather elementary, but it's related to my work."

"Oh!" Hallmark said, sensing that McIver felt disapproval, and patted him on the shoulder. McIver was the TOW platoon's gunner, probably the best in the entire division, and Hallmark, though he couldn't identify with him, knew he was a wizard. "Listen, I think this is great shit. I mean it, really. I didn't want to disturb you. Just watch your light and don't disturb folks, OK?"

McIver brightened. "Thanks, Sarge. You could play. I've got an extra toggle wired in here in case—"

"No," Hallmark interrupted. "No, not right now. I need to go see about the men, but thanks." He slid off the bench and hurried to the other side of the aircraft as McIver looked up, smiling, only fleetingly disappointed to have no challenger for the game.

Coy Vestal leaned back and rubbed his swollen lip. The bruise was coloring up well, with purple, red and yellow extending across his jaw. He was sorry Laliker wasn't on the same plane. He'd missed him on "green ramp" and was curious to see if his eye had swollen shut. He hoped it had.

In the red glow he could see Hallmark moving

25

quietly and deftly through the aircraft, locating and talking to each man in his platoon. Hallmark was checking on them, more or less taking their pulse.

He recognized Hallmark as a professional, a top-notch NCO who took his job to heart. He imagined that his own father must have been the same and again regretted having never had the opportunity to see him in action.

The posthumous Medal of Honor hung in his mom's hallway, along with the citation. He'd read it a thousand times in years past, those strong words describing incredible valor. It hadn't comforted him but had instead frightened him. An only child, he felt pressure to measure up to Dad.

Although his father and all his uncles had been Airborne, they hadn't exerted pressure on Coy to choose the military. It had been his own internal pressure.

Funny, he thought, as he gingerly touched his swollen jaw, his automatic acceptance to West Point, due to his father's Medal of Honor, had been the beginning of the animosity between him and Jeep Laliker. Laliker, a graduate from Texas A&M, had given him a hard time at Ranger school. Laliker had pushed and prodded at every occasion, chiding him for his "auto-accept" to the Point.

He had never confided his own serious doubts . . . the nagging suspicion that he wasn't cut out for this. He'd felt it all his life, every single day at the Point . . . and he felt it now as he sat in the C-141.

"Howdy, El-T," Hallmark said, having worked his way down the row of men to push in beside Vestal. "How's the lip?"

"Hurts just about as much as I deserve. Everyone OK?"

Hallmark laughed. "Yeah, just nervous. They're working it out. How about you?"

Vestal closed his eyes. "I don't know. I guess this doesn't bother you, having gone through it before."

"Bullshit. Only a fool has nothing to fear. I may be stupid at times, but I ain't no fool. No, I feel just like I did when we left for Urgent Fury in Grenada and Just Cause in Panama." Hallmark unwrapped a stick of gum and shoved it in his mouth.

"How's that?" Vestal asked.

"Oh, it's kinda hard to explain, but imagine, sir, that you're fourteen years old and someone just gave you a free ticket to a whorehouse. I mean, it's not like you don't want to go, but . . ." His voice trailed off.

Vestal laughed out loud. "Well, put, Hallmark. I can identify!"

CHAPTER THREE

The first of the Russian-made tanks, a T72M1, emerged through a thick cloud of swirling sand and ground to a halt. Following closely were twelve standard T72s and another dozen T54s which pulled in close and lurched to a stop.

The vehicles' bumpers were marked by a green triangle on a red field, with a red symbol through the triangle, the insignia of the Iraqi Republican Guard Forces. An armored personnel carrier swerved in beside the lead tank and Colonel Tariq Shadi, Commander of 2nd Brigade, hoisted himself out and onto the ground.

He beamed with satisfaction as he looked back down the road toward Kuwait City. Despite the rumbling of heavy weapons and sounds of sporadic light weapons in the distance, Shadi knew the battle was over. Flames from burning buildings reached up and licked the sky while smoke billowed from the hulks of burned-out automobiles.

His hand rested on the side of his tank. This T72M1, most advanced of the Soviet tanks available to the Iraqis, had been a personal gift from Saddam Hussein following the Iran-Iraq War. It had been a bitter consolation prize, as Shadi had not experienced a total victory. Not like the one he now savored.

Kuwait had fallen like an overripe plum. The military had been caught completely off-guard when the first Iraqi tanks swarmed over the border, and by the time they'd recovered, it was too late. Kuwait was defeated.

Shadi smiled broadly and waved both hands over his head as the crews of the tanks joined him, shouting praise for his leadership. This was worth the hardship of eight long years in Iran. Now was his moment of glory.

A young captain from Basra stepped up to him. "Allah be praised! Allah bless you for leading us to victory!" He embraced Shadi.

Shadi clapped the man on the back and pulled away. "This is not like before, Abdul. This is a fat, rich cow that we can feed on. We've waited too long for this. Tonight, the men will have everything— the women, the food, everything we should have had from Iran, for it is now ours."

A long caravan of civilian vehicles followed the tanks as they moved west of the airport. Mercedes, minivans and Cadillacs, all formerly owned by Kuwaiti citizens, now became property of the conquering Iraqi horde. As Shadi gave the men permission to return to Kuwait City, he gave no instructions for their behavior; instead, he stressed that the Kuwaitis had disobeyed Saddam Hussein for too long and must pay. Intoxicated with easy victory, Shadi now blamed Kuwait for his agony in Iran. If Kuwait had cooperated sooner, he thought,

the money would have been available to destroy
Iran. The Iraqi soldiers, too long deprived of any
luxuries, could hardly wait to dismantle the wealthy
little country.

Captain Zaheen summoned a Mercedes limou-
sine forward for the colonel. Shadi slid in, and as
his driver closed the door, he looked around inside
the spacious luxury car. A remote control panel
with buttons, custom relabeled in Arabic, was on
the armrest to his right. He hit the button marked
"Security." Immediately, dark panels rose up over
all the windows in the automobile and a shield
lowered across the front of the car, leaving a small
opening for the driver to see through. There was a
loud click as the doors and windows locked into an
auxiliary security device that couldn't be exter-
nally disconnected. Shadi laughed as he saw his
driver jump. "Don't worry, this vehicle is armored.
I want to see what measures it employs."

He left the security on and reached for the TV
button. A thirteen-inch monitor lit up on the left
side of the car, and the image of George Bush,
seated in a golf cart, filled the screen. In the
left-hand corner of the picture were the letters
CNN. An Arabic speaker translated the words of
an angry-looking president: "Yes, we have sent
contingents of the 82nd Airborne to Saudi Arabia,
and an emergency session of the United Nations
Security Council is meeting now to discuss what
other measures are to be taken. This act of naked
aggression by Iraq will not go unchecked." The
translator continued as Shadi disengaged the se-

curity device, lowering the armored shields, and looked casually out the window.

So, he thought, as the translator droned on about American congressmen protesting the President's action, the Saudis are going to oppose us. Well, no problem. They'll yield to Saddam Hussein. And America—he glanced at the screen as CNN showed a small group of protestors waving banners in front of the White House—isn't going to do anything. He flipped off the TV and eased back into the luxurious leather seat. Even their President isn't serious. He's playing golf.

By the time Shadi arrived back in the burning capital city, the Iraqi parliament had already proclaimed the area to be the nineteenth province of Iraq. To the Iraqis, there was no longer a country called Kuwait.

Hallmark was feeling cheated. The ticket to a whorehouse he'd mentioned to Lieutenant Vestal had turned out to be a rain check at best. Their C-141 had landed in Germany to refuel, and sitting on the tarmac at Rhein-Main, he'd steadied himself and the men for a combat jump into Saudi Arabia.

All so-called intelligence, not to mention hysterical rumors among the men, had indicated that Saddam Hussein would move his million-man army into Saudi Arabia. He, Sergeant First Class Van Hallmark, with a star over his master-blaster jump wings showing his combat jumps, was ready. He'd been to that "whorehouse" before. He knew the drill.

But as the plane circled to make its approach to Riyadh's airport, he felt a sinking sensation. Hallmark knew how to go in fighting, how to take on the enemy hand-to-hand if necessary, but he'd never had the job of sitting and waiting. Unsure he could handle it himself, he had his work cut out for him in keeping the morale, training, and combat edge on his men.

"Well, looks like we're going to walk in. What do you think, Hallmark?" Vestal asked, looking over at him.

"Sir, this could be the hardest money I ever earned," he replied, shaking his head as he got up to move toward the door.

The ramp lowered, and a small whirlwind whipped into the plane, scattering sand over the disembarking soldiers. The sun was high in the clear blue Arabian sky, and the temperature was 110 degrees and climbing.

"Jesus, Sarge!" Sommerhill wiped his hand across his mouth to removed the sand. "This ain't exactly paradise."

"No, son," Hallmark got behind him and pushed him along. "And watch your step here. This might just be hell."

════ CHAPTER FOUR ════

Vestal was in a hangar waiting for Captain Rodwell to finish his meeting with Battalion staff, while his platoon joined the rest of the 82nd—now hundreds of rows of bodies in the sand, trying to sleep on their rucksacks. The Saudi Arabians had provided the soldiers with large containers of drinking water, but most of the people bringing the water and hauling away empty containers were Indians or Pakistanis.

While still on the ground in Germany, the men had been briefed about the dangers of dehydration and the necessity of drinking large amounts of water. The message had been received, Vestal thought when he saw the lines of men waiting in the relentless heat to get a turn at the water containers.

A column of commercial buses queued up outside the fenced area near the hangars. He watched as the drivers, most dressed in white robes with red-and-white checked headdresses, gathered in the meager shade of their vehicles and talked with one another.

The meeting Rodwell and the other commanders were attending was in the hangar across the runway from the buses. A long line of Royal Saudi F-14 and F-15 fighters parked between the two hangars seemed do a slow, undulating dance in the heat waves.

As Vestal watched the Saudi jets dance, another C-5 landed and opened its ramp, disgorging its load of soldiers, weapons and rucksacks.

Reaction to the 120-degree temperature on the tarmac was immediate. An audible "Oh, shit!" echoed across the airstrip as the soldiers deplaned. The newly arrived commanders were met by a greeting party and quickly ushered over to the meeting hangar, while their men joined the others in the sand. There were now three C-5s on the runway. Two had already refueled and taken off for the return trip to Pope Air Force Base while the men of the 82nd watched and waited.

Loud jet screams filled the air as F-15s departed. It wasn't the perfect place to grab a nap.

An hour later, the meeting in the hangar broke up, and the Company and Battalion commanders of the 325th made their way through the swirling waves of heat, back across the runway to their waiting soldiers. Rodwell saw Vestal standing in the door as he approached and motioned him forward. Vestal moved quickly out to meet Rodwell, and they walked together into the hangar.

"We are on our way to Champion Main," Rodwell told Vestal as they entered the cool shadow of the interior. "Have your men get on the," he looked down at his notes, "eighth bus."

"Yes, sir. What's Champion Main?" Vestal asked, as Hallmark joined them.

"Saudi Arabian Air Defense Artillery site. They just finished it and we'll be the first occupants," Rodwell answered.

"What about our equipment?" queried Vestal.

"It's on its way. Just get the men settled in and we'll make arrangements."

"Eighth bus. You heard that, Sergeant Hallmark?" Vestal turned to his platoon sergeant.

"Yes, sir! Load now?"

Vestal turned back to Rodwell, who was nodding his head. "That's affirmative. Move 'em out."

Champion Main looked like a mirage on the sands. Clusters of new buildings, most of them two-story, rose from the desert floor.

"This desert is playing tricks on me, Sarge," Sommerhill said, rubbing his eyes. "I think I see grass."

"What?" Hallmark leaned forward and looked through the window of the air-conditioned bus. "Damn," he laughed, "you're right. It looks like a soccer field out there, and it is grass."

"See, maybe I was right after all. Maybe this place is paradise."

The bus came to a stop and the door flew open as Sommerhill spoke. A hot gust of air enveloped the interior, immediately sucking all the cool air out.

"Then, again," Sommerhill breathed in the dry, hot atmosphere, "I could be wrong!"

"You know, Hallmark," Vestal said as they walked

toward the buildings, "after Colonel Nix's send-off speech at Pope Air Base, about us being 'a show of force,' I was ready to jump into Baghdad—or Kuwait City—and kick ass and take names."

"Yeah, El-T." Hallmark smiled. "Me, too."

"Well, I've been doing some thinking since we arrived. Saddam Hussein has one hell of a tank-heavy army, and we're just light infantry."

Hallmark nodded. "Yeah, that's right, sir."

"We aren't even going to be a respectable speed bump if he decides to roll on over into Saudi Arabia."

"That's right, sir. Ain't it great to be part of the 'Rapid Response'?"

CHAPTER FIVE

Sounds of street fighting outside were muffled by the thick wooden doors of the villa Commander Tariq Shadi had seized as his headquarters. The villa had been the home of the Kuwaiti Air Force Commander, Doric Ben Fazid, but he didn't need it anymore. Shadi had hung him the day after Iraq invaded Kuwait. His body had swung from the rafters of the police station until the smell became so bad that the Iraqis removed it and threw it on the town dump.

Shadi made the Fazid's wife, Lyla, witness the hanging and then gave the widow to one of his tank crews for entertainment. It had been gratifying to see the high-born, impudent woman humbled and broken by repeated rape and beating. Her family was hiding, protecting foreigners and he wanted them, all of them.

During the night his men had captured her youngest son, and Shadi had sent for them both. Now, he thought, she would tell him where the traitors were hiding.

There was a loud knock on the outside door and the sound of crude laughter and jokes as two of his men entered, dragging a crumpled figure between

37

them. A soiled sheet had been thrown over the victim who seemed to hang limply between her two captors. Shadi remained seated as they dropped the covered figure in front of him and moved back.

"Get that filthy rag out of here!" Shadi said. He watched as one of the men pulled the bed sheet off the woman lying facedown on the floor.

Lyla Fazid didn't look haughty and high-born anymore. Her nude, bruised body barely quivered as they uncovered her. Shadi even flinched when he saw the outward signs of the treatment she had received.

Her hair, once long and lustrous, had been chopped off in clumps and was now matted with blood and stuck to her head and neck. Large festering burns covered her back and thighs. She moaned and mumbled something while trying to move her legs.

"What?" Shadi moved up to the edge of his chair and strained to hear what she was saying. "Turn her over."

One of the soldiers stepped forward and kicked at the supine figure on the ground, causing the woman to flip violently over on her back.

Her face had no shape. It would be hard to believe she had once been beautiful. Her nose was crushed, and as her mouth fell open, Shadi saw that her teeth had all been knocked out. Still, the cut, bruised lips tried to form a word and a low grunting noise came from the woman.

"What's she saying?" Shadi looked over to the soldier standing nearest.

"She's probably still cursing us. That's why she got her teeth knocked out." The soldier hawked and spit on her. "It doesn't make any difference, she doesn't make sense anymore."

"I told you I wanted to interrogate her. Now we can't understand her! Send in the boy!" Shadi looked down at the woman as the soldier reached to move her. "No. Leave her there. Let the son see that we mean business."

As they hurried off to fetch her son, Shadi looked at the woman lying before him. She tried to turn on her side to cover her nakedness. He felt no compassion for her, no compassion for any of the Kuwaitis. One of his tanks had been blown up by a crude pipe bomb the day before. The perpetrators had been Kuwaitis, aided, he suspected, by some of the Americans still hiding in the city.

The door opened again and Shadi watched as they led a boy of thirteen or fourteen into the room. He had been defiant as they came through the door but stopped dead still when he saw the broken body of his mother lying there. His eyes grew large with shock as he looked down at her. The soldier behind him roughly pushed him forward with the butt of his rifle, causing the boy to stumble and go down on one knee. Another of the men grabbed his hands, tied them behind his back, and yanked him back to his feet.

"Mama . . . Mama . . ." the boy called out, tears beginning to streak down his cheeks.

The figure on the floor rolled into a fetal position, pressing her knees tightly into her chest. Her arms

drew up over her head and a sob racked her
battered body.

Shadi, seeing that the boy was duly shocked,
motioned for the sheet to be thrown back over the
woman, then turned his attention to the boy.

He appraised the young man, and decided to
take a different approach. "Cut his hands free."

The bonds behind the young man's back were
cut, loosening his hands, but the soldiers held
tightly to his arms, keeping him pressed between
them.

"Where are your other brothers?" Shadi asked.

The boy looked up from the figure on the floor,
his eyes blazing with hatred through his tears.
"Did you do this to my mother?" he screamed across
the room.

"No, of course, I did not." Shadi rose from his
chair and walked toward the boy. "We tried to
question her and she resisted. She struck one of my
men. They tried to calm her down, but she hurt
herself trying to escape."

The boy shook his head, but couldn't speak.

"We'll treat your family well. We don't seek to
punish any of you, if you will just tell us where
you're hiding the foreigners." Shadi pointed to a
wooden table near the foyer and motioned for his
men to place it between him and the boy.

"I don't know what you're talking about. I haven't
seen any foreigners but your soldiers!" The young
Kuwaiti's voice was low and shaking.

Shadi reached over to his side and pulled a large
serrated knife from its scabbard. He held the knife

up, slowly waving the blade in the boy's expression-less face. "I don't wish any harm to come to you, but I must know where the foreigners are."

"I told you, I don't know!" The boy watched the blade sway back and forth.

"Perhaps you think I'm not sincere. Perhaps you think I don't mean what I say?" A smile worked across Tariq Shadi's rough features. He reached down with his knife and slammed the tip into the wooden surface of the tabletop. "Hold him," Shadi barked to the two men on either side as he grabbed the boy's hand.

He flattened the palm on the table, almost gently smoothing out each finger. "Talk to me, son. You can save your mother and yourself. All you have to do is tell me where the traitors and their foreign friends are hiding," he crooned, stroking the boy's hand.

A loud scream echoed from the villa and lingered for a moment in the hot, thick air of the alley between the buildings across the nearly deserted street.

Two men paused for a moment in their argument. Their robes and headdresses, with long trailing drapes of cloth, were the dress of the Bedouin tribesmen, nomads and camel traders who moved throughout the Arabian Peninsula.

Prior to the scream, they had been arguing fiercely over the price of a camel. Their guttural Arabic was flawless. There was nothing in their appearance or speech to betray the fact that they

41

weren't Arab. These "Arabs" were members of a U.S. Special Forces team, inserted after the invasion to help the partisans. They had been tracking the boy Ammed Ben Fazid since his capture last night.

One of the men looked around quickly to determine no one was listening, then leaned closer to the other. "We've got to get him out of here."

"I know," mumbled the other man. "Look, they're coming out now. Keep walking and arguing with me."

The Iraqi guards opened the door to the villa and stepped out in the street. One of the men carried the unconscious boy over his shoulder as two others dragged the draped figure of a woman between them. They moved down the street to the police station, talking loudly between them, as the two Bedouin tribesmen followed close behind, continuing their mock argument.

"Are we going to take her back to the house?" one asked, referring to the place where a large number of the soldiers were staying.

"No," answered the man who seemed to be in charge. "She makes the men sick. No one wants to use her anymore. We'll get a fresh one."

"Why don't we just kill them both?"

"Because," the leader answered, "Colonel Shadi wants to keep them for ransom later. They can be stored in the back of the police station. Put them in the cell there and leave a guard."

"Just one guard?" the other man asked.

"Sure. No one will know they're in there. No

42

problem," the leader said as they neared the station.

"No problem," repeated one Special Forces "Arab" to his companion as they hurriedly turned down another alley and disappeared into a mass of warehouses.

CHAPTER SIX

"Can't you just drop us by helicopter?" Jeep Laliker asked, frustration showing in his voice.

Captain Rodwell looked up from his map. "Sorry, Lieutenant Laliker, but you'll be riding with the TOWs. We'll be out for three weeks. No way we can ask for that much support from Aviation. The TOWs in our company have been selected to test with the MILES gear and we've got to support. We just don't have a vehicle for you. Your scouts will be fine with the TOW crews."

"Which TOW crew, sir?" He had sensed the answer before he asked.

Rodwell smiled. "Why, you'll be riding with 'Vestal's Virgins,' Lieutenant," Rodwell replied, referring to Lieutenant Coy Vestal's platoon. "I thought it was time you two got to know each other a little better." Rodwell stopped smiling and looked directly into Laliker's eyes. "Any problem with that, Lieutenant?"

Laliker stiffened. "No, sir."

"Good. Now get out of here and make your arrangements. I've already notified Vestal you'll be hanging on his vehicles." Rodwell turned his attention back to the map on his field desk.

Laliker stepped out of the tent into the hot desert. His BDUs were soaked with sweat but it seemed cooler now, outside Rodwell's tent. He loosened his canteen and took a sip of the warm, plastic-flavored water. As he slipped the canteen back onto his belt, his platoon sergeant, Bob Walker, approached him.

"Well, sir," Walker asked, "did you get us a truck?"

"No, Sergeant Walker, I did not. Seems we don't rate a vehicle. We'll be the guest of a TOW platoon."

Warily, Walker looked over his glasses at Laliker. "Any TOW platoon or is it someone we know?"

Laliker nodded grimly. "You got it. We'll be riding with the zipperhead and his Virgins."

"Whooeee!" Walker was grinning.

"Just save your comments and get the men together. We'll check weapons and communication at 0930, that's thirty minutes from now. Assemble and meet me at Vestal's area." Jeep was already walking toward Vestal's tent.

Coy stood inside looking out the flap as Jeep Laliker approached. "I'm not any happier about this than you are, Jeep, so just save the shit. I've got six vehicles assigned to me, two are down for maintenance, so we'll work with the remaining four to run a timed shoot with the MILES. Not only will you and your platoon be riding with us, I've got a FAC joining for the exercise."

"Life's a beach. Meet here in thirty minutes?" Jeep slipped on his sunglasses.

"Yeah. You can you come inside to wait."

45

"No thanks, Vestal. I see better company up ahead." Jeep gestured to the left.

Coy turned to see where he was pointing. A field train loaded down with mail had stopped about a hundred yards down from the tent. Stepping out of the passenger side was Colleen Harrigan. Even with it braided and stuffed under the floppy desert hat, wisps of her red hair fluttered in the wind.

"Look what just blew in from Champion Main." Laliker quickened his pace and hurried toward the truck.

"Well, I'll be damned . . . Don't be late, Laliker, or I'll leave your ass high and dry!"

Vestal had to smile as he watched Jeep talking to Colley. He'd gotten in to Dhahran their last night before departure to Training Area Romeo. By clever, covert action, he and Colley had gotten a room alone and spent the night exploring the endless possibilities of each other's body. She was an imaginative and seemingly insatiable bed partner. Vestal hadn't gotten much sleep, but what he had gotten would more than make up for it. The few times they'd been able to get together since the August landing had made the last three months of waiting almost pleasurable.

"What are you doing out here?" Jeep asked, stepping around the door in front of Colley.

"Had some free time, just thought I come out and see how the 'warriors' live." She smiled up at him. "How's it goin'?"

"Don't ask. I still haven't been able to scrounge a

vehicle, and because of this flat, see-everything terrain, they can't figure out what to do with me and my scouts."

"Everyone's complaining. Seems like we aren't doing anything but wasting time. I've been 'rumor control' for our company for the last two weeks. Some fool said we'd rotate back to Bragg for Christmas! No way." Colley looked back at the mail truck. "Have you been back at Dhahran lately?"

"Nope, just out eating sand. Why?"

"Tons and tons of mail and no way to get it out here on time. Seems like everyone in America has sent a hundred packages to help us have a good Christmas! Headquarters has every able body unloading and sorting mail. We've even done it. It's a mess." She reached up and pulled a strand of hair from her eyes. "I hear you're going out for training again."

"Yeah, train, train and train again. We're going to be out for a while on this one."

"Will you make it back for Christmas, such as it might be?"

"I think so. What's your plan for the holidays?" Jeep asked. "That is, if we aren't at war by then?"

"No plans. I go where I'm told. Why, you got something in mind?" Colley leaned forward and Jeep stepped closer.

"I'd like to see you," he said, reaching over to flick sand off her shoulder. "Think it could be arranged?"

Before she could answer, the truck driver interrupted. "OK, Lieutenant Harrigan, we're through here. You riding with me?"

"Yeah. Sorry, Jeep, catch me when you get back."
She hopped into the truck and pulled the door
closed behind her.

"You bet. Take care, Colley." He waved as the
truck pulled away from the area.

As he turned to join his scouts, already waiting
at Vestal's HMMWV, he watched a Baskin Robbins
ice-cream van stop. It was immediately bombarded
by the crowd that had assembled for mail call.

"Hell of a way to go to war. The PX ice-cream
vendors have a truck and the scouts can't get one,"
he said.

Sure that the vehicles and equipment were assembled and in place, Sergeant First Class Hallmark joined Sommerhill and McIver to pick up
their mail. He took a small bag with him and
eagerly stuffed mail addressed to "Any Service
Member" into his sack along with a pile of letters
from his wife. While McIver leafed through his
newly arrived *Computer Nut* magazine, Sommerhill argued with the mail clerk.

"You sure they ain't stacked up somewhere waiting for me?" he asked, looking around the piles of
packages and bundles of mail.

"Nope," the clerk answered, "Corporal Sommerhill, you just got those pamphlets and the one
letter. No packages."

"Let me look, then. I think you're missing something." Sommerhill edged toward the pile.

"You're not authorized." The mail clerk assumed
a defensive position over his mail.

"What's the problem, Sommerhill?" Hallmark

crossed in front of McIver and grabbed Sommerhill's shoulder.

"I *know* that Kisha's joined one of the support groups at Ft. Bragg. She told me so in her last bunch of letters, and those folks are baking cookies!" Sommerhill was moving around the packages stacked on the sand. "I ain't got *one* cookie from her yet! They got to be here somewhere!"

"There ain't no packages for him, Sarge!" the mail clerk told Hallmark. "Maybe they're in Dhahran, but they ain't on this load."

Hallmark grabbed the letters and pamphlets in Sommerhill's hand as he turned the agitated corporal around and headed him back toward the platoon assembly area. "What is this shit?" he asked, looking at the return addresses on the pamphlets, all of which were from black militant organizations. "Did you send for this stuff?"

"Huh?" Sommerhill said, still glaring back at the mail clerk over his shoulder. He swung his head around and looked down at the brochures. "What . . . Hell, no!" he said, snatching them from Hallmark. "I don't know what this is! Wait," he said, flipping through the stack, "here's a letter from Kisha. One lousy letter in six weeks!"

"Open it, son. I have a feeling it might explain your reading material."

Hallmark looked over Sommerhill's shoulder as the soldier ripped into the envelope and pulled out a single sheet with large dark scrawling. "Jeez, Sarge," Sommerhill said, as he read the letter, "listen to this. 'Dear Brother Eustas' . . . What's this 'brother' shit?"

"Read on, son." Hallmark looked down at the letter in Sommerhill's hand.

"She says," he squinted at the paper, "that she quit the support group 'cause they just wanted to make cookies . . . and wait, she's joined another group." He flipped the page over. "The name of her new group. No, it's a church group, it's 'The Sacred Southern Islam Black Brotherhood of Nebuchadnezzar.' What kind of church is that?" He looked up at Hallmark.

Hallmark shrugged his shoulders. "Beats me. She say anything else?"

"Just that she's becoming an ordained 'sister' and that she's finding a 'path.' Says it's headed up by a civilian, 'The Divine Disciple, Dr. Willie Abdul Kinzobar Johnson,' and they meet in a storefront down near the marketplace in Fayetteville."

Hallmark closed his eyes. He remembered the area around the marketplace in downtown Fayetteville. It had been one of those "abandoned because of funds" restorations done in the 1980s and was now a long line of defunct stores, wig shops and havens for drug traffic. Not a great place for a church or, he thought, perhaps the perfect place for one. "Anything else?"

"No." Sommerhill wadded up the letter and stuck it in his pocket. "Just that she's put me on a mailing list so I'll have something to read and think about. She didn't even say she loved me."

"Well," Hallmark patted him on the shoulder,

"she's probably just worried and busy. Lots of different ways to relieve tension, you know. Wives have it worse than we do. They don't know what's happening over here, so they worry. Don't let it get to you."

"I liked her other letters better. She said she missed me, and all the games we used to play." Sommerhill looked up. "I'm sorry, Sarge. You know, 'games' is what we called—"

Hallmark interrupted. "I think I know what 'games' means." He smiled and pushed the mailbag into his rucksack. "I may be thirty-six years old, and divorced, but I remember 'games.' She'll shape up. Get on over there and start your HMMWV. We need to get going pretty quick."

He nodded and stuffed the rest of his mail into his BDUs. Sergeant McIver joined Hallmark.

"How's it going?" Hallmark greeted the team leader as McIver shoved his magazine into his pack. "You getting lots of support mail from home?"

McIver looked up, squinting through his thick glasses, which seemed permanently coated with a thin film of sand. "You forget where I'm from, Sergeant Van? Do you remember that recruiting commercial that starts out 'This is not like my hometown'?" McIver snapped. "Well, my hometown is full of gutless pukes that hate everything our once well-respected nation ever stood for! They're money-grubbing real-estate fascists all week and knee-jerk postcard-writin', street-marchin' pinkos on the weekend! No, I don't get much support from my little northern California hometown, and I don't care, 'cause I hate 'em!"

"Harold," the SFC said, raising an eyebrow.

McIver clammed up, but an unspoken tirade showed, still building pressure. "Sorry," he said, "but I get a little steamed about home. Glad the rest of the country seems to have its head on straight."

Looks are certainly deceiving, Hallmark thought, staring at McIver's red face. It was the first time he'd seen that kind of fire from the computer whiz. His fascination with machines and seemingly passionless nature had always puzzled Hallmark. He could never understand why McIver was in the 82nd, why he'd gone through jump school and Ranger training. For the first time Hallmark could identify with McIver, and the realization surprised him. McIver, Hallmark marveled, was a high-tech "rompin', stompin' Airborne Ranger," a new variant of an old breed.

"Here." Hallmark reached inside his ruck and pulled out some mail. "Take these." He selected two of the "Any Service Member" letters and handed them to McIver. "They're from Texas. You'll find some support there."

McIver, the color subsiding in his face, accepted the letters and looked down at them. "I don't know if I have time . . ."

"Oh, you've got time. That's all we've got out here, and too damn much of it. By the way, where's the new guy?" Hallmark referred to Private First

Class Michael Neuhaus, a recent addition to the platoon.

"He's with Sommerhill. I'll let him train with Eustas on this exercise and hopefully, if they get the other HMMWVs fixed, make him a driver. What do you think?"

"Works for me. What's he like?"

McIver shrugged. "Who knows. He's quiet, seems like he's educated, more than just high school. Knows a little bit about computers, so we fool around with them some, but he's not a big talker. Comes from upstate New York but gets no mail, never mentions a family."

Hallmark rubbed the stubble on his chin. "Well, looks like we're ready to move. out. I'll ride with your bunch."

Vestal's four functional M996 HMMWVs were lined up waiting to go, the M-220 TOW missile systems mounted on top. Each squad had ten missiles on the HMMWVs, filling the tubes, with extras attached to the sides. Intelligence reports warned of the possibility of Iraq's Russian-made tanks, T72M1s, detecting the earlier TOWs, so a new series, the Delta model, immune to the detectors, had been hurriedly sent over. When and if they ever went into action, Vestal's crew would carry both the old C series and the new D series.

For this exercise, an External Evaluation or EXEVAL, the squads loaded six MILES missile simulation rounds, each with an ATWESS (Anti-tank Weapon Effect Signature Simulator) cartridge,

AIRBORNE

into the missile storage racks. The MILES system
used laser light to simulate actual weapons fire.

Vestal rode with Hallmark, McIver, Sommerhill
and the new man, PFC. Neuhaus. The Air Force
Fire Control Officer and his RTO hopped in with
them while Jeep Laliker and a few of his scouts
made room for themselves and their weapons on the
ammo racks. A second HMMWV followed with the
rest of the scout platoon.

CHAPTER SEVEN

Vestal leaned back and shouted to Laliker, "This is as far as we go. Everybody out!" The HMMWVs stopped and unloaded Jeep Laliker, his scout platoon and their equipment. Vestal didn't even look back as his vehicles took off, leaving Jeep and his men in a swirl of sand.

"Sir," SFC. Bob Walker, Laliker's platoon sergeant, motioned him over, "I think there's some mistake here." The men walked toward them as Jeep looked at the map in Walker's hands.

"What?" he said, looking over the sergeant's shoulder. "What mistake?"

"We're here, sir," Walker indicated a spot on the map. "That's forty miles from where we should be! We got off too soon."

Jeep spun around toward the departing HMM-WVs. "Vestal, you bastard!" he yelled, as the vehicles, far beyond earshot, disappeared behind a thick veil of sand.

Walker reached over and grabbed him by the shoulder. "They can't hear us. Don't upset the men, sir."

Laliker continued to stand there, staring out at the swirling sand, fighting for composure. Finally he turned back around to his platoon. "OK," he said, nodding at Walker, "we'll be testing commo equipment. Our purpose is to move forward and be the eyes for the rest of the company and stay out of sight so the eyes and ears of the Marine Recon, who are acting as the aggressors, don't pick us up. So, let's get out there and look like moving sand dunes and camel shit!"

The two TOW units sped back to join their waiting "Hunter-Killer Bees" as the scouts headed out on the barren plain some hundred and fifty kilometers from the border between Iraq and Saudi Arabia.

The sun hadn't waned in these last days of November, and the temperature hovered at the 110-degree mark. Everything was difficult in the heat, but the MOPP gear, protective clothing and masks, in case of chemical warfare, made the difficult almost impossible.

The goal of this EXEVAL was to achieve realism using artillery simulators, smoke grenades and tear gas. To add stress to the gunners, the engagements would be timed.

The Saudis had donated a line of burned-out automobiles for targets. They were placed in a random pattern across the lip of a small rock outcrop.

As Vestal's HMMWV pulled into formation, the FAC (Forward Air Control) called in a "fire mission" and four artillery simulators blasted in front of them.

McIver, Vestal's gunner, grumbled as he yanked

on the MOPP gear. It was difficult enough to track the target at 2,000 meters, but it was worse as he tried to fit his protective mask against the eyepiece of the sight. The platform was unstable, wobbling wildly as Sommerhill made his turn for the firing.

The target autos were downrange. McIver received his orders and engaged the first target at 1,000 meters, not knowing when the artillery or gas would be added to his problem. There was a fiery burst as the missile made contact. He turned quickly to the next target, at 1200 meters, and fired. The time elapsed was thirty seconds. The target flamed and rolled on impact.

Sweat poured down into his eyes, stinging and causing him to blink rapidly. Third target lined up in the cross hairs, and he fired. Sand was now swirling and blowing heavily, obscuring McIver's vision even more. As the missile fired, several resounding pops banged against the HMMWV. Thick billowing clouds of smoke began to cloud up around the vehicle as the smoke grenades erupted. Time elapsed: fifty seconds. The pressure was on McIver now as he struggled to find the fourth target. He tried to adjust his eyepiece as the sweat poured into his eyes.

"Son of a bitch!" he exclaimed, as he fired at the target. It was at 3,000 meters. He missed. The next target was 3,330 meters away. He could barely make out the shape in the cross hairs as he locked and fired. He missed again. He hit the button for the last missile, and this time, he made contact.

Time between the fourth and fifth target was sixty-five seconds. He was late, had a complete miss and a second fire on the last target.

The HMMWV started up and made a wide arc back to the secondary firing position as the second squad moved into firing posture. The other three squads would test before Vestal's crew would fire again.

There was no time to evaluate as the squad reloaded, but McIver knew it hadn't been good. He took a deep breath and looked down at his hands. The adrenaline was wearing off, and the shaking lessened as he watched them. "Chill out," he said to himself. His neck, covered with heat rash, was burning, irritated by the clumsy MOPP headgear.

Vestal stepped over to him. "Steady, McIver. What's happening out there?"

"No excuses, El-T. Just gotta adjust to the atmosphere and gear. We'll smoke 'em next round."

"You heard him, Sommerhill! We loaded and ready to run?"

"Yes, sir," he shouted, and everyone fell back into position in the HMMWV. They pulled out and prepared for the next firing.

Vestal was worried. If McIver had had a bad run, the other gunners would do worse. McIver was his best. The sand was stirred and providing a thick tan curtain now between the targets and the gunners, further complicated by the smoke grenades and tear gas. The fake artillery steadily bombarded them with simulated rounds, completing the worst conditions Vestal had ever trained under. It was a "worst case scenario" firing.

Hallmark was watching with intense concentration. He didn't give a damn about the rounds, the high-tech measuring devices checking their accuracy or the high-speed officials watching the firing. His interest was focused on the performance and morale of the men. He was pleased. The more hellish the conditions became, the better they performed.

Give them hell, and they become devils, he thought. He new this wasn't actually a "worst case scenario"; it could get much worse. The true "worst case" was when the targets were firing back.

McIver delivered on his promise as the squad made their next firing, and the other squads were markedly better the second time around. As the results came in, McIver had an all-time high accuracy of 90 percent, even with his first firing averaged in. Vestal's Virgin's were doing all right.

Accuracy tests over, they returned to Romeo, and the checking and cleaning of equipment began. As Hallmark checked on the fifty-caliber guns mounted on two of the HMMWVs, Vestal talked with the FAC.

The Air Force officer was from Georgia and had a deep "Southern-fried" quality to his speech. "Not bad, Lieutenant Vestal. Your boze seem to cotton to this heat right nicely!"

"Yeah." Vestal looked out at the men as they carried out the task of settling in. "They're a good bunch when they have something to do. I wish we could do live firings every time we went out."

"I know what you mean. We've had our share of trouble back at headquarters, too. This just sittin' 'round makes ever'body real edgy. Congress, back in the States, is arguing now about givin' the President the authority to use force. Hell, we still don't know if they're gonna decide to load all our little asses up and send us home tomorrow."

"I spend more time breaking up fights and disciplining bored troops than training. We can't just sit here in the sand with nothing to do, but today was great." Vestal said, as he offered the Air Force officer a stick of gum.

"Thanks," he said, accepting. Pre-softened by the heat, it stubbornly stuck to the paper as he worked it off and into his mouth. "This place, this Arabia, is like sittin' on the sun itself. Man, I would give anything for a good ol' November Georgia day, heavy clouds, mebbe a little rain . . . hell, just a quick chill in the air! I guess I'm just gettin' a little nostalgic."

Vestal laughed. "Hell, we've all been here too long! Come on, I can't buy you a beer, but I've got a couple of Gatorades my mom sent over in the HMMWV."

"Let's go pop those tops!"

They returned to the HMMWV, got the drinks and found some relief from the sun under Coy's shelter half. Within the hour a helicopter swooped in, picked up the FAC and his RTO and returned them to Riyadh. Vestal got busy with his own tent and stowed away his things.

Hallmark finished his rounds, got his tent set up and sat down on his camp stool to read his mail. His ex-wife, Gloria, was good about writing. He regretted the divorce, but she couldn't stand the separations. It had started with the trip to Grenada; they talked divorce before Panama, but by the time he got home from Operation Just Cause, the talking had stopped. The marriage was over, at least legally. Somehow, he just didn't feel like it was over, and from the letters she kept writing him, it seemed she didn't either.

There were some pictures of their three boys, dressed in their soccer uniforms. The oldest looked just like her; her blue-green eyes blazed back at Hallmark from the photo. The boys didn't understand, but then, what was there to understand? He loved her and she loved him, but their lives couldn't mesh. She wanted an eight-to-five, home-on-weekends kind of man. Constant security. He couldn't live that way. He loved her, loved the kids, but he loved the life he lived, too, and knew he wasn't going to change.

He read news of the boys, how they were doing in school, family gossip, and that the dog had had eight puppies. Gloria swore they all looked like poodles, and that was strange since their dog was a German shepherd. The letter ended with a question: "If we could try again, would we make it? All my love, Gloria."

Well, Hallmark thought to himself, now there's a

situation that could use some considering. He closed his eyes and eased back on the stool. Yeah, that's a question we should work on.

The rest of his mail was from schoolchildren across the United States, expressing support and love. He pulled out some paper and started answering the letters, all of them except Gloria's. That one would take a little more time.

McIver opened the letters Hallmark had given him. One was from a ten-year-old in Odessa, Texas, who ended the letter with "I said everything my teacher said to say. Now I can say what I think. I wish I was there so I could help you KICK ASS!"

McIver laughed and folded the letter, then slipped it into his pocket. He'd answer it later. The second letter was from a woman in her forties. She expressed pride and support for the actions so far and wished him luck in the days ahead. As he read on, he found she was the widow of an infantryman killed in Vietnam. She said she didn't expect McIver to write back, she knew he was busy, but to "keep your head down, your powder dry and your spirits high." McIver was moved by her support. He left his tent in search of stationery and felt good to have the letters to answer. It was nice to know the whole country wasn't as nuts as his hometown.

Everything, including the blowing sand, settled as the day ended. Camp was set up quickly, and the schedule of simulated firings for the next ten days was posted. Hallmark made his way through the men, encouraging, discouraging and generally making sure that their fighting edge stayed sharp.

• • •

Jeep Laliker and his scouts had a whole different set of problems as they moved forward against the elements. He pressed his men hard, pushing them to complete thirty miles across the hot, dry terrain before coming to a place to camp. They were going through their canteens at a rapid rate. The first day of any exercise was always the most difficult, and this was no exception. The pace was six miles an hour, and in the heat, it was deadly. Commo checks were set up on a random basis, and to date, all Laliker had communicated was his position. The rendezvous and designated checkpoints to measure their effectiveness had to be adjusted for their location. Arrangements were made to resupply them with water and food for their extended trip.

Laliker's objective would bring him within twenty kilometers of the Iraq border. A Marine Reconnaissance unit was somewhere up ahead, and the scouts were to locate them, report back their position and observe them, undetected, as part of the exercise. The Marines had commo equipment also, so Laliker kept radio transmissions to a minimum, to avoid giving away their position.

At the end of the march across the sand, the men were hot and thirsty, but, to Laliker's relief, they were still in good spirits. There was only sporadic grumbling about the heat and a few newfound blisters as the men set up camp.

"Dig yourselves into the sand about two to three feet," his first sergeant instructed the men, "and

63

use your shelter halves for a roof. This desert gets real nippy at night. Once the sun goes down, you'll remember what it's like to be cold. Oh, and watch out for those crawly things. All the snakes out here are poisonous . . . and the bugs, too, and they all hunt at night. We won't be patrolling tonight, so get some rest."

Laliker and his first sergeant found a place for their "two-man foxhole" and pulled out their entrenching tools to dig in.

"Tomorrow's going to be a bitch," Laliker said, throwing a spadeful of sand over his shoulder.

"Yeah, let's try to get at least twenty out of them before noon, get down and out of the sun until dark, then push for another five hours while we don't have the sun on our backs. Our water resupply hits here at 0400 hours. I figure we're up and ready by then and pull out as soon as we've filled up. Don't worry, sir. The men don't know we're out too far. We'll be in position and do well on the exercise."

CHAPTER EIGHT

The loud blast across the street knocked the guard to his knees. As he struggled to right himself, he realized the blast had come from the building where his company was quartered. The door to the police station had blown open with the impact and smoke and sand billowed in from the street. Suddenly there were several more blasts in the street, loud, but not with the impact of the first explosion.

Grabbing his AK-47, the guard rushed through the open door into the street. Before he could reach the burning building across from him, his eyes began to burn. Too late he recognized tear gas emanating from one of the detonated rounds. The gas cut off his air and he choked—hard.

As he choked and fell to the ground, a short burst from an Uzi made sure he wouldn't get up again. Two more Iraqis stumbled toward the police station through the thick smoke and were cut down by the deadly fire. Still cloaked in their Bedouin disguises, the two Special Forces men waved their weapons, signaling a group of men at the corner to move forward. The group, all armed with Uzis and AKs, rushed down the street and into the police station.

"Where are they?" asked a large man as he pushed past the Americans and into the small office.

"In the back cell. Quick, let's get the hell out of here!" came the reply.

From down at the end of the alley they heard another loud explosion, part of a planned diversion to provide cover while they picked up their prisoners.

"Ammed! Ammed!" the large man called out, as he led the others toward the back of the station. "Where are you?"

He heard a low groan as he opened the door to the cells. In the dim light he could make out one figure lying on a cot and another trying to pull up to a standing position on the cell floor.

"Omar?" The voice responding was weak. "Omar, is that you?"

"Yes, brother, I am here. Where is our mother?" The Kuwaiti moved quickly to the cell and opened the door with the keys he'd grabbed from the desk outside. As the door swung open, the boy fell into his brother's arms.

"I didn't tell them anything. I didn't tell them where you were," cried the younger man into his brother's chest.

Omar looked at the blood on Ammed's face. The boy had been beaten badly. Over Ammed's shoulder he could see the still form on the cot.

"She's near death," Ammed said and pointed toward the cot, dropping the blood-soaked rag he'd held tightly around his right forearm.

Omar gasped. His little brother's right hand had no fingers.

He had no time to react before one of the Americans shouted to him down the hall. "We gotta go . . . *Now!*"

The woman, covered with a thin cotton blanket, moaned. Omar watched as the Americans carried her past him. She looked like no one he had ever seen before, nothing like the quiet, beautiful Lyla Fazid. His brother was being carried out as Omar passed the Americans guarding the door.

His anger made it difficult for him to speak. The Special Forces sergeant in the door pushed him on down the street and hurried after him.

An Iraqi jeep screeched around the corner. Before the two Iraqis could take aim, a partisan fired his RPG at the jeep. The grenade struck the windshield and exploded, hurling the two passengers into the street. Another explosion rocked the building where the Iraqi troops were quartered. The building whooshed into flames. Pieces of debris rose high in the air, then plummeted back down to the now vacant street. The partisans, their American advisors and the prisoners made their getaway in the smoke and confusion.

The jeep hit by the RPG lay on its side, smoldering. A large fiery piece of debris fell from the burning building and hit the jeep, igniting the gas tank and sending pieces of flying metal and fire down the length of the street.

A Soviet BMP-1 fighting vehicle, followed by a platoon of Iraqis, rounded the corner, ready for action, but the enemy was gone, leaving only flames, bodies and wreckage as their calling card.

Tariq Shadi heard the explosions. He scrambled for his weapons as one of his lieutenants opened the door to the large study. "Sir, there's fighting down the street. We have sent two platoons."

"Where down the street?" Shadi asked, as he walked to the hall door.

"Near the police station, I think," the lieutenant answered.

Before he got to the door, his adjutant, Captain Abbenz, rushed down the hall to meet him. "Sir, it was the Kuwaitis again. They blew up a building where some of our troops were housed."

"Did we catch them?" the Iraqi tank commander shouted.

"I . . . don't know, sir. I don't think so," Abbenz said, watching warily as the commander turned and walked toward him.

"Find them, or bring me twenty Kuwaitis to die in their place. Let it be known, after you have rounded up the group, that we will have a public execution in two days. Perhaps that will dampen their spirits."

Hidden in the warehouse district near the port, a Kuwaiti surgeon labored over Lyla Fazid's broken body. He shuddered as he viewed the brutality the woman had been subjected to. She would live, her body would survive, but he knew, looking into the dull eyes that stared back at him, that her mind was gone. He finished cleaning and binding the visible wounds, rigged a sling to alleviate the pressure on her broken shoulder and dabbed gently at the bruises on her face.

The Special Forces medic had supplied him with a syringe of morphine for her, but he hadn't used it because he was unsure of the head injuries she'd sustained. It hadn't mattered; Lyla Fazid was beyond pain. He turned to the small table beside him and washed his hands. There was no more he could do for her.

The American medic cleaned the boy's hand and wrapped it in sterile bandages. The Iraqis had done the boy a cruel favor. After they'd chopped off his fingers, they'd cauterized the stubs. They hadn't wanted him dead, just maimed.

"How's it going?" the SF team leader asked, bending over the medic's shoulder as he worked with the boy's hand.

"He's a tough little customer," the medic replied. "I've seen grown men faint when they get an injection. Hell, this kid helped me work on his hand."

"You OK?" The team leader looked at the boy.

"Yes," the boy answered in English. "I want to help you fight."

"And you will, son, you will. Just not here. We need to get you to the border and into Saudi Arabia."

"I don't want to go. This is my country, these are my people. I can fight, even with one hand."

"No doubt about that, but the Iraqis are looking

69

for you now. We need for you to get out of here and tell the Saudis and our people what's going on. It will do more for your people than anything else."

"What about my mother?"

"We'll get her out, too, as soon as she's able to travel."

"And my brothers?"

"Omar will go with you, but the others will stay. We have work to finish here."

Omar was standing near his mother's bed when he heard his name. He walked over to his younger brother. "She's very weak," he said. "When do you want us to go?" He looked up at the Special Forces sergeant.

"Does Dr. Nabid think she can walk?" the sergeant asked.

"Yes, she can walk, but she needs some rest. Maybe in two days," Omar answered.

"You've got twenty-four hours, and that's taking some big chances. Transportation is being worked out now with some herdsmen. We can get her on a camel for part of the way, but she'll have to be able to move on foot, if necessary."

"We will do what is required." Omar nodded. "Thank you. If I could have a few minutes with my brother now . . . ?" Omar asked, staring at Ammed's gauze-wrapped hand.

"Sure," the medic answered for them. "Just keep that hand in the sling, OK, Ammed? And keep it hidden under this robe," he said, draping the material over the boy's shoulder.

The two Americans turned and walked down to

join a group of men at the other end of the building, leaving the Fazid brothers alone to talk. Omar cleared a spot on the table and sat down next to Ammed.

"You understand why we have to leave, don't you?" he asked, switching back to Arabic.

"No! . . . Yes . . . I don't know, Omar. What has happened? Why is our father dead? Why did this happen to our mother?" The boy, aware that the Americans couldn't see him now, began to weep.

Omar reached over and put his arm around his brother, pulling him close. "Easy, easy, it's all right. I don't understand either. Maybe we won't ever understand, but we must live through this. We must survive."

"I thought the Iraqis were our friends," the boy sobbed.

"Yes, and that the Americans were our enemy. It looks like we were wrong."

"Mother . . . did you see what they did to her?" His sobbing became deeper.

"Yes, but believe me, Ammed, we may go to Saudi Arabia now, but we'll come back to Kuwait, and when we do, the Iraqis will pay for what they have done!"

The Special Forces sergeant stood next to the medic and looked down the warehouse at the two brothers. "Damn, this makes me sick."

"Yeah, but at least we got these guys out in time. Now if we can only get them out of here."

71

"The boy seems fit and ready to go. What about the woman?"

"We're pushing it by moving her, but she'll make it. Hell, she doesn't even know where she is anymore. She'll never have her mind back, but the body will function."

The sergeant stubbed out his Moroccan cigarette and looked at the medic. "Get them ready to move out in the morning. I've got to get down and check out the details. See you back here in two hours."

"Be careful out there. The traffic is hell," the medic said, smiling, as the other man pulled the edges of his burnoose close to his face and stepped out into the Kuwait sunshine.

CHAPTER NINE

"Do you realize how far they have to go to get to their objective?" Captain Rodwell asked, glaring at Vestal.

"Sir, their objective was unclear to me at the time." Vestal stood ramrod straight in front of Rodwell's camp desk.

"Hell, Vestal, I think that's bullshit! I think you dropped them off knowing full well that they were fifty miles from where their exercise started! They don't even come into the zone of detection by the Marines until they hit that mark! I'm having to resupply with water trucks until they reach that zone!"

"Sir, I was concerned with my TOW firing mission. I'm not a scout, sir, and Lieutenant Laliker didn't fully inform me of his exercise."

"Vestal," Rodwell held the stub of a cigar tightly clenched in his teeth as he spoke, "I've just about had enough of this petty rivalry between you and Laliker. You may be one 'hotshot' TOW commander, but you aren't much of a team player. This is a *combined* effort here; we all have to work together. There's not room for a couple of egos to fuck with each other!"

Coy watched as Rodwell paced angrily behind his desk. A rivulet of sweat ran down between Vestal's shoulder blades, causing him to flinch.

"Yes, sir, mister," Rodwell continued pacing, "if I could prove you did this on purpose—which I *know* you did—I'd court-martial your ass!"

Vestal didn't say a word, didn't move a muscle. He knew he was in trouble. It was a stupid stunt and he'd regretted it from the first, but he'd done it.

"I've got twenty scouts out there, walking in this god-awful heat, and if any of them come back in here on stretchers, I'll hang you. Do you understand—they better not even get a blister, or I'll have you breaking rocks at a federal prison!" Rodwell removed the cigar. "You are a fucking disgrace to your father's name. Get out of my sight, and you better be praying for the well-being of Lieutenant Laliker and his platoon."

"Yes, sir!" Vestal snapped a salute, wheeled around and exited the tent.

Hallmark was standing by the HMMWV as Vestal came out of the tent. Rodwell's voice had carried, and he hadn't missed a word of the chewing out. Anyone within thirty feet of the tent would have heard it.

"Start her up, Eustas," Hallmark said to Sommerhill. "I think the El-T needs to make a quick getaway."

"No shit! We're out of here!" Sommerhill turned on the ignition.

"Let's get back to camp," Vestal said, sliding past

Hallmark into the seat. Hallmark nodded, jumped in and closed the door.

The rode in stony silence down the sandy highway toward their camp. Vestal stared out the window of the HMMWV, lost in his misery.

Hallmark suddenly snapped his head around to the lieutenant. *"Vestal* . . . Of course, John Vestal, your old man, was a Special Forces medic . . . won the Medal of Honor in Vietnam."

Vestal's jaw clenched. "Posthumous award."

"Damn . . . 'Scuse me, sir." Sommerhill looked over at the man sitting between him and Hallmark. "My old man was over there, too, two tours. With the 101st, though."

"Yeah?" Vestal continued to look straight ahead. "I had a couple of uncles with the 101st. You come from an Airborne family, too."

"Uh-huh . . . but we only jump because of the extra pay," he responded, stealing a glance at Hallmark.

"I never met your old man, but I sure did hear about him," Hallmark continued, oblivious to Sommerhill. "Some of my friends went to the Special Forces medical course when he was instructing. He was one hell of an NCO. One of the legends of the Airborne. He served time with the 82nd, too, didn't he?"

"I was born at Womack when he was in the first brigade," Vestal answered.

"Yeah, yeah . . . that's him." Hallmark reached in his pocket for a cigarette. "I'm trying to remember how the citation for the Medal of Honor

75

read . . . seems like it was . . . something about going back in after he was gravely wounded—"

Vestal interrupted. "And pulling out three more of his comrades who had fallen under the intense fire. He put them on the stretchers and loaded them on the helicopter, then held off the North Vietnamese advance, so the chopper could get away." Vestal seemed to slump into the seat. "He sacrificed his life to get the wounded out of the area. They never recovered his body, but the medics in the chopper saw him fall under heavy fire from the enemy as they flew out. There was no doubt that he was dead."

A deep silence followed when Vestal stopped speaking. All three men looked straight ahead at the road that stretched out in front of them.

Sommerhill reached down and pulled his Walkman from under the seat. He plugged in the earpieces and escaped into the dull thud of rap music on the tape. He thought he'd had trouble living up to his old man's Silver Star.

Man, he thought to himself, being Lieutenant Vestal, the son of Medal of Honor winner Master Sergeant John Vestal, must be a bitch.

Hallmark stared down at the unlit cigarette in his hand. He placed it between his lips and reached for his lighter.

"Those things will kill you, you know," Vestal said, turning to face him.

"Almost everything I do will kill me eventually, El-T," Hallmark said, sparking the lighter and taking a deep drag.

"Not to mention running around with stupid lieutenants, huh?" Vestal said, staring straight ahead. "You heard what happened in Rodwell's tent?"

"Yep." Hallmark exhaled a thin blue puff of smoke. "I heard."

"Well? It's not like you to spare a critical comment."

"The only sin, if we survive our mistakes, sir, is ignoring the lessons they teach us." Hallmark took another drag. "I've watched you and Laliker go after each other for months now. I figure it's all good training for a new career when I retire from the military."

Vestal turned his head and looked directly at Hallmark. "New career?"

"Yeah," Hallmark said, flipping the cigarette out the window. "I figure I'm well trained, by you two, to manage a nursery school. You asked, and I'm gonna tell you. This shit's got to stop. This is no place for children—you two better grow up before you get some good men killed."

He had it coming and he knew it. Vestal didn't respond at all. The words stung, but truth does that. He turned his thoughts to Laliker and started doing some of the praying Rodwell had told him to do.

It was day three, and the last water supply truck had left two hours ago. Laliker and his first sergeant had signaled a thirty-minute rest.

"He had to have known he'd dropped us off too

77

soon. He had to have known!" Laliker wiped the grit from his mouth as he spoke.

"Give it a rest, sir. We're doing all right. We're where we're supposed to be, now. I've ordered radio silence so the Marines won't be able to pinpoint us."

"How's morale?" Jeep asked. "Are the men doing OK?"

"Yeah, sir, they're fine. They're actually doing better mentally than they do back at Champion Main. They like getting out here and doing their work, even if they bitch about it among themselves."

"I can understand that," Jeep answered. "Nothing is worse than just sitting around with nothing to do. I get pretty nuts myself."

"Yes, sir," SFC. Walker said, taking a sip from his canteen. "We all do."

A large group of boulders, protruding like aliens from the sand, provided the scouts with some much needed relief from the sun. Jeep eased back and rested against one of them.

"God," he said, sniffing around, "do you smell that? Something must have crawled up here and died." He looked around, still sniffing.

Walker laughed. "Yeah . . . I smell it."

"Well," Laliker said, turning toward him, "what is it?"

"Us, sir, it's us."

Laliker sniffed again. "It is us!"

"You better believe it! I think I'll just burn these BDUs when we get back to Main." Walker raised his arm, pretended to take a whiff and grimaced. "This is no way for a civilized human being to smell."

"You know, last night in the foxhole, I thought it was you!" Laliker laughed. "I guess that's why we didn't get any visits from the snakes or scorpions . . . We gassed 'em!"

"Chemical warfare, at its worst! We better get movin', sir. We got a 'rendezvous with destiny'!" Walker rose, stretched and shouldered his rifle.

"That we do, Walker, that we do," Jeep said. "Signal the men. Let's go get 'em."

Walker nodded and walked down to get the men up and moving. The platoon fell in and dispersed across the sand, using the rock outcrops when possible for both shelter from the sun and to avoid detection by the Marine recon.

Jeep moved up and fell in beside Walker. "Actually, you know," he said, adjusting his pace to the sergeant's, "this heat isn't really all that bad."

Walker tilted his head and looked over the top of his glasses at the lieutenant. "No, sir, not if you were raised in Hell!"

"Hell? No, not exactly *Hell*. In fact, lots of people call it Heaven . . . I was raised in Southwest Texas. Why, I had heat rash before I had diaper rash! Nope," Jeep walked along, chewing a piece of gum, "I don't find this heat all that bad."

"Well, sir, it don't feel a thing like Maine, where I was raised. Not a minute of it." Walker adjusted his ruck. "Have you ever been up there?"

"Nope, not really. I guess we might have flown

out of Bangor a few times on our way to Europe, but I never got to see much, except through the window of an airplane."

"Your family military?" Walker asked.

"All the way! Why a Laliker has been in every battle our country ever fought. Even had relatives on both sides in the Civil War. You might call the Army the 'Laliker Family Business.'"

"Not mine. I'm first-generation American. My family was Scottish. Immigrated to Canada in the late 1800s. My dad came down to the States after World War II and married my mom in Portland. He's a fisherman. My family on both sides, both Mom's and Dad's, have been fishermen. I was the first soldier."

"You didn't like fishing?" Jeep asked, spitting out his gum.

"No, I like fishing . . . I just didn't like working for my older brothers." Walker reached up and flicked sand off his glasses. "I guess you grew up wanting to soldier, huh?"

"That's right." Jeep smiled. "I guess so anyway. It's the only thing anyone in my family ever talked about. I tried to get an appointment to the Military Academy, but I didn't. Really disappointed my dad. He was in the class of 1946, third in the class. My grandfather was in the class with MacArthur. Everyone went to West Point but me. I ended up going to Texas A&M."

"Well, that's not shabby!" Walker commented.

"It wasn't," Laliker agreed. "I was corps commander. Did real well, but it still isn't up to par, as far as Dad's concerned. He pinned his old 'butter bars' on me at graduation, though." Laliker cleared his throat nervously. He hadn't meant to open up as much as he had.

"He ever say that to you, your dad, I mean?" Walker asked.

Laliker reached into his pocket for another piece of gum. "No, but I know he's disappointed."

They walked along in silence for a while. Laliker stripped the paper off the gum and flipped it into his mouth. "That's what burns my ass about Vestal," he said, chomping down on the gum. "His old man's Medal of Honor gave him an automatic in to the Point. He didn't have to put out any extra effort, and he just skates through life! What a prick!"

"I don't know," Walker said, moistening his lips. "He had no dad standing there at his graduation and you did. I loved my old man. I still remember all the fun we had when I was growing up . . . fishing with him . . . tramping out through the woods in the snow. I miss him. Lieutenant Vestal missed that . . . missed learning at the old man's knee. I believe you and I got the better deal."

"You're pretty philosophical, aren't you?" Laliker quipped.

"Fishing the Atlantic, sir. That'll make a man do a lot of thinking. I guess it does make one philosophical."

Laliker looked over at Walker. His rugged profile, his freckles gleaming through the redness of his sunburn—it wasn't hard to imagine him on the bow of a fishing boat, facing the fury of an Atlantic storm.

"Your old man must have been great," he said, smiling, "and probably wise, too. Seems like he passed some of it along to you."

Walker laughed. "He was a good man, sir, but I don't know how wise I am."

"Well, in some things you are, Bob, but you forgot to put the sunscreen on back there, and your fair Scottish complexion is turning bright red. Better be taking care of yourself as well as taking care of me." He handed a tube of the sunscreen to Walker, and they continued on as Walker liberally applied the lotion.

CHAPTER TEN

McIver sat on a camp stool in the tent, busily working on his laptop computer. The click of the keys beat a steady rhythm in the room. He listened to the radio while he worked, a set of earpieces jammed in his ears. In his own world, he was completely unaware of anything or anyone else in the tent.

PFC. Mike Neuhaus lay on his sleeping bag, arms behind his head, and stared at the tent ceiling, listening to the clack-clack of McIver's computer keys. He swung his arm down and looked at the steel Rolex on his wrist. The date was November 29, and the time was 11:45. Just a few minutes till lunch. He folded his arm back behind his head and continued to lie there.

His thoughts took him back to upstate New York. He wondered if the folks had had a nice Thanksgiving. They always went to the cabin for the holiday. His mom even cooked. Since it was the only time during the year she tried her hand at culinary skills, the meal was always a surprise. His sister had started smuggling cans of beef stew in her luggage for the trip, so if all else failed, they could at least eat. He remembered a few platters of beef stew.

Those were the good times, before the fights, before he quit Harvard. Before his father, Michael Fitzwater Neuhaus III, had thrown him out, forbidden the family to have any contact with him, disowned him and told him not to use their name. He could hardly change his name, but he had dropped the IV after Neuhaus. That had been two years ago, and he hadn't heard a word from them since. Nothing.

A few of his friends had written, mostly out of curiosity, when he went to boot camp. They soon grew bored with the oddity of having one of their circle in the Army, and the letters had ceased. He knew his sister had divorced and was living at home again. He'd tried to get in touch with her, but all his letters had been returned, unopened, marked "Return to Sender" . . . in his father's own unmistakable handwriting. The phone numbers at the house had been changed and unlisted. When he'd tried to reach his dad to tell him he was leaving for Saudi Arabia, his father's secretary had briskly told him not to call again.

Yep, he thought to himself, when the old man said there was no way back, he meant it.

"Whoa!" McIver slammed off the computer and turned to Neuhaus. "The United Nations Security Council just voted to authorize all necessary means against Iraq if it doesn't withdraw . . . *Whoa!* Wait a minute . . . Saddam's got a deadline . . . He has to be out by January 15th!" He yanked the earpieces out and turned up the volume. High static interfered with the transmission, but the

AFN disc jockey, Milton Pope, kept repeating, "UN Security Council's message: Saddam, you better get out of town by January 15th!"

Neuhaus sat up. "Wait . . . What does that mean?"

McIver turned down the volume. "It means *use of force*! It means if he don't move, we move him!"

"Then we might be doing more than training?" Neuhaus asked, looking at McIver's excited face.

"That's the message!"

Through the static the Armed Forces DJ continued to read the news release. "The UN also cautioned Saddam Hussein to observe the Geneva Protocol that bans all use of chemical weapons."

"Yeah, like he's really going to do that!" Neuhaus reached down and tied the laces on his boots. "I believe Bush when he said Saddam's never had a weapon he hasn't used. He gassed the Kurds a while back!"

McIver nodded. "That he did. I heard that he killed five thousand of them, his own people."

"Well," Neuhaus said, as he stood up, "I don't think he'd have any qualms about using them on us."

"We'd be his *second* target, if he decides to blow some gas. I figure Israel would be his first. It would certainly give him some clout with his Arab brothers, some of which are in this coalition. God knows the Arabs don't like us, but they *hate* Israel."

Neuhaus reached over and picked up his MOPP headgear. "I hate this shit," he said, shaking the ugly head covering, "I really do."

85

"It's going to feel like an uncomfortable second skin before this mess is over. I'm going out to find Hallmark. I wonder if he's heard about this." McIver left the radio on as he rushed out of the tent.

Hallmark was near the field train, waiting to draw his T-rations for the men and talking to Lieutenant Vestal, as McIver ran toward them. "Been listening to the radio?" he asked as he neared them.

"Just heard," Vestal responded. "Guess that'll slam-dunk the rumor that we're going home for Christmas."

"Is AFN reporting on the reaction in the States to this news? I wonder how it's sitting with 'Cid Civilian' and the great American Congress." Hallmark waved away a horde of sand gnats swarming in his face.

"Didn't listen long enough," McIver said, "but it sounded like it was too fresh to get any public reaction."

"Too bad we're not back at Main. I imagine the media pukes are all over the place looking for our reaction," Vestal said, looking past McIver as Captain Rodwell walked toward them. Rodwell stopped and motioned Vestal over.

Vestal hurried over and stood in front of the captain. "Yes, sir?"

"There seems to be some news from your friend, Lieutenant Laliker. Thought you might be interested, since you've got a lot at stake here."

Vestal felt a tight clench in his stomach. "Yes, sir, I am interested."

Rodwell flashed an amused smile. "He found the Marines yesterday, successfully, and started back last night. I was considering having you go out to pick him up, but it seems it isn't necessary. He's hitched a ride with some Bedouin tribesmen and is on his way in."

Vestal's face was still blank. "That's good news, sir."

"I thought you'd be pleased, but there's more. It seems he has some refugees with him."

"Refugees?"

"Seems the tribesmen helped smuggle out some Kuwaitis. They're in need of a medic, so we sent a group forward to meet them."

Vestal's complexion went ashen. "A medic?"

Rodwell watched Vestal's reaction. "For the refugees, Vestal. Lieutenant Laliker is a fine officer. He met his objective, despite an obstacle thrown in his way, and got all his men back safely. I'm damned proud to have him in my command."

"Yes, sir, Lieutenant Laliker is a good officer. I'm glad everything went so well."

"I knew you would be, Vestal. I'm going to be meeting with him within the next hour. I have a decision to make and I thought you might help me with it."

Coy shifted his feet uneasily. "Yes, sir."

"Good, good." Rodwell slapped him on the back. "Let's get out of the sun and I'll tell you about it."

Hallmark and McIver watched as Vestal followed the captain across the encampment.

"What's that all about?" McIver asked, watching as the two officers disappeared into Rodwell's tent.

"Word is that ARAMCO, the big oil company over here, is asking to have deserving platoons come in, as their guests, and spend a week on R&R," Hallmark said. "Rodwell was told that he could select one of his best for Christmas."

"Hot damn! That's us! We fired better than anyone else last week. He'll send us." McIver smiled broadly.

"Not so fast, Mac. I'm not sure we'll be in the running."

McIver's smile faded. "What do you mean 'in the running'? We're the best!"

Hallmark scuffed the toe of his boot on the sand. "There might be other factors at work here. Just don't go announcing anything till the El-T says so."

Sommerhill came running toward them. "Hey, Sarge! I hear we're going to be the guests of ARAMCO for Christmas! The clerk down at the 'head shed' said we're it 'cause we're so damned good! Ain't that great! I mean we're gonna get VIP treatment, home-cooked meals, real people to talk to—civilian types—sleep in beds, with *sheets*, sleep as long as we want, unlimited phone calls home! Man! This is gonna be great!"

McIver looked at Hallmark. "Looks like I won't have to make any announcements. I think everybody knows already."

"Damn!" Hallmark turned on his heel and walked

over to the field train. "Come on, help me get these T-rats. I think we got lucky here and are having lasagna." Under his breath he muttered, "Except for El-T. He's eating crow!"

"What's the matter with him?" Sommerhill asked as he watched Hallmark leave. "I thought he'd be happy as hell. I *am*. Now I'm gonna call Kisha and get some shit straightened out!" He danced around in front of McIver. "Maybe . . . just maybe we'll get to talk some trash . . . This is great!"

McIver looked at Sommerhill and shook his head. "Don't go countin' on it, Eustas. Hallmark isn't near as sure about this as you are."

"Well, fuck him if he can't be sure! I am. I already heard it from four different sources! We got it bagged! See you later. I got to go tell some of the others."

Sommerhill was off so fast McIver couldn't stop him. He watched as Eustas grabbed everyone he passed, spreading the news.

God, McIver thought to himself, walking over to help Hallmark, I hope it's true.

CHAPTER ELEVEN

The HMMWV carrying the medics pulled to a stop as the caravan approached it.

"Hey, Sarge," the driver asked, "you sure this is the right place? Look at that grid again."

The sergeant sitting next to him looked down at the map in his hands. "We're where we're supposed to be. That must be them."

"Well, it don't look like no scout platoon to me! Looks like a bunch of camel and goat herders." The driver looked at the approaching caravan and back down at the map in the sergeant's hands.

As the caravan drew nearer, one of the figures riding a camel stopped. The camel knelt to let the man dismount. The men in the HMMWV watched as he swung his M-60 into view and dropped off the animal's back.

"Must be our boys. Even in these days, I don't think the Bedouins are carrying M-60s and dressing in chocolate-chips," the sergeant said, turning toward the medics in back. "OK, message says we got refugees hurt bad. Let's go do our job. See what the damage is and I'll call in the chopper."

The medics jumped out of the HMMWV and hurried toward the BDU-clad man walking toward them. He motioned to the last three camels in the convoy and continued walking toward the vehicle as the medics rushed past him.

"Glad to see you," Jeep Laliker said as he reached the vehicle. "Got anything to drink in that machine, other than water?"

The sergeant reached down and handed him a Pepsi. "Yes, sir, and it's *cold!*"

"Oh, man." Jeep rested the M-60 on the side panel of the HMMWV and grabbed the can. "I don't know if my system can take it. How long before the chopper gets here?"

"It's on its way. It was in flight as I called in. I figure they're twenty minutes out."

The other members of the scout platoon were working their way forward. Laliker turned and yelled for them to drop smoke to guide the chopper in.

"What did you pick up out there, Lieutenant?" the driver asked, squinting to see where the medics were opening up the stretchers.

"Five Kuwaiti nationals, three of whom are in need of medical attention. The worst of them is a woman, but there's a kid with missing fingers and a man with a gunshot wound in the shoulder. The man and the boy are less critical, but the woman is in bad shape."

"Bad shape?"

"Yeah." Laliker turned and spit in the sand. "She must have had every bone in her body broken."

"Shit!"

"Wait till you see the kid. They chopped off all

91

the fingers on his right hand—one at a time—
trying to make him talk." Laliker watched as the
smoke from the chopper rose up around them. "The
woman is his mother."

"How did you get all that information? You got a
translator?" the sergeant asked.

"Nope, the kid's brother is with them. Speaks
good English, but then he should, he graduated
from UCLA. Their last name is Fazid, part of the
ruling family of Kuwait. I figure Intel will swarm
around these folks when we get them back. They'll
have a lot to debrief. Seems like they were assisted
out of the country by a bunch of our Green Berets."

Loud *whappa-whappa* sounds filled the air, signaling the arrival of the chopper. The convoy of
camels, along with their herds of goats, moved
quickly away from the area, their animals reacting
nervously to the sound of the incoming helicopter.

Lyla Fazid's stretcher was carefully lifted and
placed in the chopper. The medics carried the IVs
they'd rigged for her and continued to work as they
boarded. Omar and Ammed climbed in, along with
the man with the shoulder wound and the other
escaped partisan. Laliker and his platoon opted to
ride back to the training area in the now empty
HMMWV.

"So," Walker said, looking over at Laliker as they
sped across the sand, "what are you going to do
about our 'short drop'?"

Jeep continued to stare out over the HMMWV's
abbreviated hood. "Something . . . You better believe, I'm gonna do something about it." The mus-

cles around his jaw jumped as he clenched his teeth. "Vestal isn't gonna skate on this."

"You know, it's gonna be hard to prove he did it on purpose."

"It doesn't matter," Jeep answered. "I know he did it, and he knows he did it. And it's not going to end here. No, not yet."

═══ CHAPTER TWELVE ═══

"They're on their way in, Vestal. I think you ought to be out there to welcome them back," Rodwell said, walking into Vestal's tent. "Laliker and his platoon rode in on the medic's HMMWV. They should be here in about thirty minutes." He saw Vestal sitting on the camp stool, bent over with his head in his hands.

"Yes, sir." Coy jumped up and stood at attention. "I'll be there."

"By the way, I just heard that members of your platoon are running around camp telling everyone about their reward R&R with ARAMCO. Maybe you better tell them what you decided." Rodwell stood in the entry, glaring back at Vestal.

"I thought you were going to tell them, sir," Vestal said.

Rodwell snorted. "Oh, no, Lieutenant Vestal. You are going to tell your men. That's part of the punishment. They'll give you the rest of it after they hear . . . and, mister, whatever they say to you, you have coming." He turned briskly and left Vestal to ponder his fate.

Vestal took a deep breath and ran his hand over his head, feeling the stiff bristles from his last haircut. He reached down and buttoned his BDU blouse. "Hallmark!" he shouted through the open tent flap.

"Sir?" Hallmark had been on his way to see Vestal when he saw Rodwell enter the tent. He had stepped back and given the captain time to leave.

"Assemble the men. We're going to meet Laliker's platoon. I need to make an announcement concerning the reward R&R, and I'll make it after Laliker arrives. It concerns him, too." Vestal slipped on his sunglasses and stepped outside.

"Sir," Hallmark said, "if this is what I think it is, I can tell them. They aren't going to take it too well."

"No, I don't imagine they will." Coy ran his tongue over his parched lips. "But I'm the reason and, therefore, the one to make the announcement." He reached over and cuffed Hallmark on the shoulder. "Thanks, but like Rodwell says, 'It's part of the punishment.'"

Laliker could see Vestal standing in front of Hallmark and his platoon by the side of the road. They were about three hundred feet away from the encampment. Vestal called his men to attention and turned to face them as the scouts came to a stop a few feet away.

"The purpose of this assembly," Vestal said to his platoon, with the scouts looking on, "is to congratulate you on your EXEVAL. This platoon had the highest accuracy rate of all TOW units in the battalion. Your professionalism and proficiency gained the attention of higher headquarters, and you will be given two days of R&R at Champion Main upon our return, followed by two weeks of training there at Main."

A grumble went through the TOW platoon. "What's this 'two days at Main' shit?" Sommerhill said though the side of his mouth.

"You're at attention!" Hallmark barked at the assembly.

"The platoon with the highest overall proficiency, however, is Lieutenant Laliker's scout platoon. They earned a week at the ARAMCO compound, as guests of ARAMCO and their families."

A shout went up from the scouts, now out of the HMMWV and standing next to Laliker.

Vestal continued. "The competition was rated in all areas—proficiency in accomplishing the mission, accuracy and leadership. The one area we fell short in was leadership. And the fault is mine. That's all, men. Dismiss them, First Sergeant."

Sommerhill was beside himself. "What the *fuck* happened? We had it bagged! It was that damned stunt of the El-T's, wasn't it?" He looked over at Hallmark, his face a mix of disappointment and fury.

"Out of here, Corporal! Put a lid on it!"

"What 'stunt'?" McIver sidled up to Sommerhill as they walked away.

"The El-T dropped the scouts short of their exercise! He was fucking with Lieutenant Laliker! One fucking officer playing games with another fucking officer and we lose a holiday leave! That sucks!" Sommerhill said, in a voice loud enough for everyone to hear.

Vestal hadn't missed it, or any of the other derogatory comments issued by the men of his platoon. He would just keep his face straight and act as if he hadn't heard it, because, as Rodwell had pointed out, he deserved everything the men said. Laliker joined him and glared into his face.

"It isn't enough," Laliker growled, "you sorry shit! It isn't enough!"

"Laliker, I'm here to tell you the bullshit between us has stopped, as of now. I'd like to shake hands and start over." Vestal offered his hand.

"Just like that, huh? You tried your best to screw up my mission, endangered my men . . . and you want to shake hands and start over? You can go to hell!" Laliker shouted, turning his back and leaving Vestal with his hand still extended. "Sergeant Walker, get the men into camp. Something stinks out here and I don't want them contaminated."

Vestal withdrew his hand and continued to stand there as everyone pushed past him into camp. He sighed deeply. Well, he thought to himself as he turned and walked slowly back in, I have one hell of a lot of work to do.

CHAPTER THIRTEEN

The ride back in to Champion Main didn't seem very long to Vestal. His platoon spent their time talking with the scouts about the rescue of the Kuwait refugees. Laliker's stock had risen enormously in the Battalion, while Vestal's star was tarnished.

Other Battalion lieutenants had stopped by Vestal's tent prior to departure for Main, to express disbelief that he would do what they'd heard. Vestal refused to discuss it with them. It was obvious to him, as he sat next to PFC. Neuhaus on the ride in, that they had drawn their conclusions and didn't want to have anything to do with him. He closed his eyes and leaned his head against the window.

"Excuse me, sir," Neuhaus said, looking over at Vestal, "are you asleep?"

Vestal opened his eyes. "No, Neuhaus," he said. "What's on your mind?"

"Those Kuwaiti nationals that Laliker's scouts found. They are really having a hard time up there in Kuwait, aren't they?"

"The Iraqis aren't known for their benevolent treatment of prisoners," Vestal said. "Back when we were supporting Iraq in the war against Iran, stories came out about the atrocities they performed against captured Iranians. Of course, we didn't pay too much attention to it then. After all, Iran was our enemy, too. Iraq is not one of the most humane countries in the Middle East."

"I was talking about this to Sommerhill," Neuhaus continued. "He couldn't believe it . . . I mean, we expect them to cut us no slack, but the Kuwaitis were friendly to Iraq . . . gave them money, helped them before. I mean, it's like Sommerhill said, they're all Muslims."

"Yes," Vestal said, "but remember, Saddam Hussein is a Baathist. They are nondenominational, recognizing neither Christian nor Muslim, in their party. The Baathists are nationalists, defiant nationalists, with only one mission in mind, to establish Iraq's supremacy in the Arab world. That's almost as important as their vowed intent to destroy Israel. There's no room for brotherhood in that mission."

"Hussein is calling for all the Arab nations to join him in destroying us, and Israel."

"That's what he'd like to see happen."

"Do you think it's possible? You think our new Arab allies might turn on us and join with Hussein?"

"Jesus, Neuhaus," Vestal exclaimed, amused by the private's intensity, "*I* don't know! What were you majoring in at Harvard, International Politics?"

"No, sir, International Law." Neuhaus moved nervously in his seat.

"Law?"

"Yes, sir."

"There's some big international law firm in New York City, Neuhaus, Klepper, and Somebody, I believe. One of my roommates at the Point dated a legal secretary that worked for them. You related to that Neuhaus?"

Mike Neuhaus looked down at his hands. "I . . . was, sir."

"Was?" Vestal glanced over at him. "That's a strange comment."

"I'd rather not discuss it, sir, if you don't mind."

Vestal continued to stare at the man next to him. "No, there's things I don't want to discuss, either." He turned and looked out the window. "You like the Airborne, Neuhaus?" he asked.

Neuhaus brightened. "Yes, sir, I really do, all things considered. It's challenging. I needed that. I still get nervous when we jump, but I like it."

Vestal laughed. "Me, too. I wish we could get a few jumps lined up over here."

While Neuhaus and Vestal shared jump stories, Hallmark and McIver, in the seat in front of them, went over training changes.

"Sommerhill is pushing me for a promotion," Hallmark said, opening the notebook he always carried in his pocket. "He's not going to get it as a driver. I'd like to shift him over to gunner, put Neuhaus in as driver. What do you think?"

"Neuhaus will make a good driver . . . I don't

know about Sommerhill as a gunner. He's a real whiner, if you now what I mean." McIver watched as Hallmark scribbled in his book.

"Now, Mac, he's a good man . . . He's just confused. He pays attention to detail, though, and he's got good reflexes in a clinch. Do you think you could train him?"

"Given the time and opportunity, I could train a dog to fire the TOWs. Yeah, I'll work on it." McIver sighed and leaned back in the seat. "He don't like me, though."

"Sommerhill likes you . . . He hates the fact that he does, but he likes you. Don't let that aggressive 'homeboy' facade he's put up fool you. He's one hundred percent professional. I'll stake my stripes on it!"

McIver nodded, not totally convinced. "Well . . . if you say so. What about me?"

"Oh, I guess I forgot to tell you. You're out of uniform, Staff Sergeant! Get that new stripe sewed on when we get back to Main, or I'll give it to someone who appreciates it," Hallmark said, feigning seriousness.

"No shit!" McIver sat up straight in the seat. "OK!"

Riding along in the back of the bus, Walker watched as Laliker pulled a package out of his ruck and began unwrapping it.

"Don't tell me," he said, as Laliker picked up one of the several long, thin chains with tiny coins attached to them. "That camel jockey *did* sell you that thing! What are you going to do with it, send it to your mother?"

Laliker laughed out loud, jingling the coins in his hand. "No, I don't think dear old Mom would wear this belly dancer's outfit, but I know someone who will. Can you believe that Arab had a charge plate for my MasterCard?"

SFC. Walker chuckled. "Sure, they probably had a run on charge plates when they heard the 82nd was on its way over here! How much did that outfit end up costing you?"

"You mean, *after* the haggling?" Jeep shook his head. "I'll never tell, but if I get to see this thing on the person it's intended for, it'll be worth every red cent I paid." He pulled out a bra made of tiny chains and coins. *"Every cent!"*

"By the time you get back to 'the world' to see that thing, your fantasy might be better than the reality," Walker warned.

Laliker turned and smiled broadly. "Hey, Walker, the object of my affection is a whole lot closer than 'the world,' and when she sees this, she'll make the arrangements for a private showing."

Walker reached over and shook the package of chains. "Just in time for the holidays, eh, sir!" He listened as the coins banged merrily together. "Jingle Bells, Jingle Bells!"

"Ho! Ho! Ho!" Jeep laughed.

The scouts, all seated near Jeep and the first sergeant, joined in the revelry and soon were leading the entire bus in Christmas songs, both original versions and bawdier renditions, made up by the men as they drove on toward Champion Main.

Vestal heard them, but didn't join in. His platoon wasn't singing either. Sommerhill turned around and scowled at him as the loud singing rang through the bus. Coy resumed his position against the window with his eyes closed, avoiding the corporal's accusing glare.

CHAPTER FOURTEEN

Word of the UN Security Council's decision to place a deadline for the Iraqi withdrawal had not eluded Colonel Tariq Shadi's attention. He sat in the den of the large Fazid villa, watching CNN on the thirty-six-inch screen across the room. He impatiently stubbed out his cigar and shouted for his second in command, Lieutenant Colonel Abdul Bareem. Bareem hurried in from the foyer.

"Sir!" He snapped a salute as he came to a stop by Shadi's chair.

Shadi hurriedly returned the salute and motioned for Bareem to sit in the chair across from him. "I think we need to make some plans, just a few precautions, in case we need them," he said, as the lieutenant colonel sat down.

Bareem leaned forward in his chair. "Yes, Colonel Shadi. What have you got in mind?"

Shadi pointed to an area on the map lying in front of them on the coffee table. "I think we should move all of the T72s along with the T64s— no, all the tanks, along with their crews. Send some of the infantry companies with them. I want underground bunkers prepared to house the tanks and crew members."

His second in command stared at him with curiosity. "All the T72s?" he asked.

"Yes." Shadi nodded his head, still looking at the map. "All of them." He sat back, looking at Bareem. "It's just a precaution."

Bareem looked over at the TV and back to Shadi. "Has something new developed?"

"Not really," Shadi answered. "Just that the American-controlled United Nations took a vote today, a stupid move, but I'm annoyed that the only three negative votes came from Cuba, Yemen and China. I'd feel better if our Arab neighbors would show their support."

"They don't have the benefit of our great leader," Bareem said, his voice full of confidence.

"Hmmm." Tariq continued to study the man sitting across from him. "I also want everything stripped from this house, all dishes, appliances, all the personal possessions of the Fazid family loaded up and taken to the bunkers. All these things are now mine."

"Yes, sir. I'll have the men get to it first thing next week." Bareem veiled his surprise at the commander's personal request.

"No!" Shadi stood and walked to a large silver coffee service on the buffet. He reached over and lovingly caressed the beautifully worked sterling pot. "Not next week, Bareem. I want the tanks out of here today, and I want the work to start immediately on the bunkers. The house will be packed for shipment tomorrow and sent out to the bunkers, with the exception of the silver and jewelry.

I'm sending them to Baghdad tonight in one of the Mercedes parked in Fazid's garage."

"Yes, sir." Bareem watched as his commander walked around the room, admiring the works of art hanging on the walls.

"Just look at this, Abdul! These things should be in Baghdad." He stopped and bent over to examine the pattern in a large carpet at his feet. "Silk." He turned, smiling with wonder. "It's silk! These are truly the rewards to a conqueror! I have earned these, and you have, too."

"You are most generous, sir." Bareem glowed. "I do see some things in the quarters I occupy that I'd like to send home."

Shadi strolled casually across the marble floors, back to his chair. "Then take them, have them packed with my own. And I'd like for you to have the other Mercedes in the garage." Tariq seemed to enjoy the power inherent in handing out trinkets to his faithful. "But," he said, returning to his stern composure, "be sure these things are loaded and out of here tomorrow."

"Yes, sir!" Bareem rose from the chair. "I'll get to it right away. Anything else, sir?" he asked as he stood, smoothing his tunic.

Tariq had folded his hands and was resting his chin on them. He looked up at Bareem. "The traitors seem to continue to be a problem. Are you continuing the executions?"

Clearing his throat, Bareem nervously replied, "Yes, twenty citizens are executed daily, as per your instructions. I think things are being made clear to the rest now."

"I don't think so, Bareem. They're still attacking our guards at night, sabotaging our vehicles—they are still resisting." Tariq lowered his hands into his lap and leaned back in the chair. "Double the number. I want forty executions a day for the next ten days. Make it well known, use their TV station to tell them."

Bareem stood in the doorway, ready to leave. "Yes, that can be done. When do you want to start?"

Shadi continued to relax in the chair with his eyes closed. He raised an eyebrow.

"Why wait?" He laughed. "Start today. And Bareem," he said, as the man started out, "I want to be moved to the villa at the edge of town . . . I think some of your captains are occupying it now. I can hardly live here after tomorrow, can I?"

===== CHAPTER FIFTEEN =====

"Welcome to Dhahran. Make yourself comfortable while I slip into this thing," she purred, disappearing down the hallway into the master bedroom.

"Sure you don't need some help . . . I mean, those things have a thousand tiny adjustments that need to be made," Laliker said hopefully. "I'd be glad to help."

"You're *too* kind, generous sir!" she yelled back through a closed door. "I think I'll let you do the adjustments after I get it on."

Jeep yanked off his desert cap and slapped it against his leg, scattering sand on the hardwood floor. He was enjoying the air-conditioning and looked around at the large living room with its cathedral ceiling. There were a few cushions on the floor, scattered around a hammered brass tray. The size of the otherwise empty room made them look like miniatures, even though the pillows and tray were quiet large. "Any of these places come furnished?" he shouted down the hallway to the master bedroom.

He could hear the jingling of the belly-dancer outfit and laughter coming from the room. "No! At least not that I know of" came the response.

"Damn, Jeep, this thing is wild. I'm not sure I'm really going to wear this out of this room!"

"Then," he called out, "I'll just have to come in there to view it! You promised you'd model it for me."

"Stay where you are! I intend to make good on my promise. I'll be out in a minute. There's some orange juice in the fridge."

Laliker walked into the kitchen. The flooring was marble, the appliances top-of-the-line.

"Glasses are in the cabinet left of the sink," called the voice from the hall.

Laliker took a glass and placed it in the slot in the door, then pushed the button marked "Ice." Immediately large round dots of ice filled his glass. "Class," he said to himself, pouring juice over the ice and listening to it crackle.

He took a sip of the cold beverage and walked back into the living room. As he lowered himself onto one of the pillows, he unbuttoned and removed his BDU blouse. "You sure we aren't going to be disturbed?"

"Yes," she said, "my roommates have their instructions. Besides that, one of them is pulling duty for me. We've got until midnight." There was a pause, then, "This is taking longer than I thought it would. Just relax. I'm about done."

Laliker looked down at his watch. It was thirteen hundred hours. He smiled. "Till midnight," he said to himself. "OK!"

Through the sliding glass door to the balcony, he could see the bright blue water of the Persian Gulf.

Her apartment was in one of the Kobar Towers, an attempt by the Saudi Arabians to provide housing for the Bedouin tribesmen. The Bedouins, traditionally tent-dwelling nomads of the desert, hadn't wanted the towers. After the project was completed, it was abandoned because the tribesmen chose to continue their nomadic way of life. The Saudis had turned the buildings over to the U.S. forces and allies to use for billets. Here was the crème-de-la-crème of U.S. military housing in Saudi Arabia.

After unlacing and removing his boots, Jeep stretched out and lay back on the cushions. He sipped the last of the juice and yawned. He was totally relaxed and comfortable for the first time since he'd gotten off the plane in August. Yes, sir, he thought to himself, this is the life. He closed his eyes and was about to doze off when he heard the bedroom door open and the sound of clinking coins and tiny bells coming from the hallway.

He rolled over on his side and watched as an arm, thinly covered in deep green chiffon, waved back and forth like a cobra ready to strike.

"I hope you're ready for this!" a feminine voice said from its still-concealed position. "I haven't got any music to dance to so you'll have to hum or something."

"I'll just breathe heavy! Come on out here and quit teasing!"

Colleen Harrigan moved sensuously into view, undulating her hips and causing the bells and coins to jingle madly. She held her hands over her head, palms together, and slithered into the room.

The chiffon pasha pants and the bra of chains and coins concealed nothing as she swayed and moved across the room like a cat.

Her red hair, freed from the French braid, floated like a flaming silken cloud on her bare shoulders. She arched her back, and her long hair dusted the floor as her body, twisting and shaking, bent backward.

Laliker reached out to grab her, but she shimmied away quickly, laughing. Laliker yanked off his socks and stood up to take off his BDU pants. "I can't take anymore," he said, dropping the last of his clothes on the floor. "Either dance your beautiful ass into the bedroom now, or I'll do you right here on the floor!"

Colley smiled, throwing her head up and extending her arms. "Well," she said, "the floor seems fine . . ."

It was dark in the bedroom when Laliker rolled over and looked at the luminous dial on his watch. This room, like the others, was unfurnished, but the opened sleeping bags had been an improvement after the hardwood floor. The dial on Laliker's watch glowed 20:35. They had been asleep for over two hours.

He folded his arms behind his head and lay there, staring up at the ceiling in the dark. Colley, awakened by his movement, reached over and slid her hand across his chest, then snuggled close to him. "Hi," she murmured sleepily. "You awake?"

"Uh-huh," he said, lowering his arm and drawing her tighter to him.

They continued to lie there, enjoying the warmth of each other's body. Colley stretched out and eased up on one elbow.

"What are you doing?" she asked, looking over at Jeep.

"Thinking about what a rough life an Arab sheik has," he replied, continuing to cradle her in his arm.

She ran her a hand through the tangles in her hair. "Rough life? How do you figure that?"

"Well, I figure I'm in fairly good shape . . . being Airborne and all . . ."

"You are," she interrupted, running her hand down the length of his torso.

He shivered as goose bumps ran up and down his skin. "Hey," he grabbed her hand and continued. "But these guys have as many wives as they can afford, and dancing girls, too!"

"Yeah." She laughed, trying to yank her hand away. "So how does that make their life rough?"

"Trying to satisfy all those women, that's how! God, I feel like you've used me up, and you're the only *one* woman. I don't think I'd make it!"

"Oh yeah? Well, maybe this wasn't a true test 'cause remember, your belly dancer is Airborne, too! I can't believe you're saying you couldn't make it!"

"I think it might be heaven for the first week, but after that, I'd be dead with a smile on my face . . . if they were all like you."

112

"Hey!" Colley pulled away and stood up. "There is *no* other me. You should know that by now." She reached into the walk-in closet and pulled out a short red silk robe.

"What are you doing? I thought you said we had until midnight?" He raised himself up on both elbows and watched as she tied the sash.

"Calories."

"What? What do you mean 'calories'?"

"It's time to replenish our depleted calorie banks. In other words, I'm starving." She padded off down the hall, and he heard the clink of a pot as it hit the stove.

Jeep stood up and found a towel to wrap around his waist. "Well," he said, stepping out into the hall, "if you're going to cook, I'll take a shower."

Colley leaned around the kitchen doorway into the hall. "Cook? You must be kidding. I don't cook for nobody, and if I did, there's nothing in here to fix. I'm making some tea to go with my MREs."

"Somehow I *knew* that. Oh well, I'll take a shower anyway and join you in a minute."

Colley listened to the shower come on in the bathroom. Clothes were scattered all over the living room, along with various pieces of her dancing outfit. While Jeep showered, she picked up their things and put them away.

He stepped out of the shower and dried off with an Army-issue towel. Colley had tossed his clothes on the countertop. "Hey," he said, picking up his T-shirt and slipping it on, "does this mean I'm supposed to get dressed?"

"Yep," Colley answered, her mouth full of date cake. "I want to go see Gerald McRaney and Delta Burke. They're gonna be at the headquarters parking lot at twenty-two hundred hours."

Laliker pulled on his BDU pants and walked into the kitchen as he buttoned them. "I kinda thought we'd stay here . . ."

She peeled the foil wrapper back on the cake for Jeep to take a bite. "I want to see some celebrities! Save it. There'll be a next time."

"You sure about that?" He cocked his head.

"Sure, I'm sure."

He took a bite and reached up, holding on to her wrist. "Will you wear the same outfit next time?"

"No, you've had me as a dancing girl. Next time I'll be Scheherazade, and tell you long, sexy stories until you quiver."

"Deal!"

Colley laughed and went down the hall to shower. She continued to talk as she turned on the water. "Did I tell you I saw Steve Martin when he was here?"

Jeep couldn't understand her over the shower, but it didn't matter. He heard her chatter mixed with the splashing water as he walked out onto the balcony. Thousands of stars twinkled in the dark sky, like a diamond-and-velvet canopy hung over the waves of the Persian Gulf.

Colley was great, the sex had been incredible, but he felt as if something were missing.

"You coming with me?" She was dressed and stood, impatiently, in the doorway.

"Would it matter?" he asked.

"Sure," she said, smiling, as she reached for the doorknob. "I'd miss you."

Somehow, even after their intimacy of the afternoon, he didn't quite believe her.

CHAPTER SIXTEEN

Coy Vestal had not had a good night. Earlier, he'd looked for Laliker, hoping to talk and smooth things over, only to find he'd gone into Dhahran for the night. He visited the makeshift dayroom and watched CNN for a while but grew bored as they interviewed one retired World War II general after another. Sitting there, he noticed that none of his peer group had anything to say to him. They walked around him as if he weren't there.

It was morning now, and he put on his shorts, T-shirt and running shoes for the daily D Company run. The men were already in formation as he walked over to join them.

"Mornin', Hallmark," he said. "Ready to go?"

"All the way, sir!" Hallmark leaned over and touched the ground with his fingertips, stretching out his hamstrings.

"I want some 'Jody' calls this morning."

"Sommerhill! Count cadence!" Hallmark yelled over his shoulder.

"Maybe not, Van," McIver whispered to Hallmark. "He's still pissed at the El-T."

Hallmark opened his mouth to respond, but Vestal started off in the Airborne shuffle. The rest of the platoon fell in behind him.

Sommerhill's voice, deep and resonant, sang out each line of the cadence as the men repeated.

"The Airborne is a way of life!" Sommerhill rang out.

The platoon repeated as they shuffled along. "To earn more money and lose your wife!" As the group repeated, Hallmark's skin started to crawl, anticipating the corporal's next lines.

"You go new places to get new thrills!" A smile was on Sommerhill's face as he listened to the repeated refrain.

"You meet new people that you can kill!"

Not bad, Hallmark thought, relaxing somewhat.

"Vestal had his Virgins go!" began the next stanza. "To the desert to fire their TOW!" They rounded the circle as the platoon shouted back the line.

Sommerhill's crooked smile widened. "To the sand the scouts got trucked!" He had become louder.

Before Hallmark could figure out a way to stop him, the platoon had repeated.

"A little bit short so the gunners got fucked!" There was no pause as the platoon, less Hallmark and Vestal, repeated.

"Neuhaus! Count Cadence!" Hallmark yelled, stopping Sommerhill. The other platoons and companies passing them didn't hide their amusement. Vestal stared straight ahead and continued the run.

"Corporal Sommerhill!" Hallmark stood at rigid attention as he spit out the words. "You want to know why you don't get promoted? I'll tell you why . . . 'cause you're *stupid*." He leaned forward, his nose almost touching Sommerhill's as the corporal stood in front of him.

"Yes, Sergeant!" Eustas knew he'd gone too far, but he was angry, and he wasn't going to back down.

"You better believe 'Yes, Sergeant!'" Hallmark straightened up and put his hands on his hips. "I don't know how you got to be a corporal."

"You promoted me." Sommerhill's eyes blazed as he answered.

"This is no time to wise-off. I'm making a decision about you, right now, and your smart mouth is unduly influencing me, if you know what I mean."

Sommerhill remained silent, but his eyes were still hot.

"You'll do garbage detail this morning. I want you to make sure there isn't one single cigarette butt on this entire Champion Main. You've got an hour before we start classes, so get moving."

Sommerhill cut his eyes at Hallmark, tempted to say one more thing, but he thought about it and remained quiet. He turned on his heel and moved away.

"Taking a pulse on morale?" McIver had been leaning on the side of a building, listening.

"Yeah! It's off the charts," Hallmark said, walking over to join him. "Training will be a bit dicey this morning."

"You are the master of understatements, Van. Where's the El-T?"

"Over getting his daily ration of dog shit from Captain Rodwell. Did you check on the mail situation?"

McIver shrugged. "No mail today."

"Great. That's just fuckin' great." Hallmark ran his hand over his head. "No mail, low morale, lousy MREs, and we're stuck here training in classrooms for the next three weeks."

"That's not all," McIver said, watching as Sommerhill picked up butts across the track from them. "We had several folks fall out for sick call this morning."

Hallmark turned and spit into the sand. "You're shittin' me."

"No," McIver replied. "Seems they felt sick after the run."

Hallmark looked over at McIver. "You know, if the El-T wasn't so busy kicking himself in the ass, I think I'd kick it for him. Well, come on, Mac, let's see if we can salvage this day and get some work done."

CHAPTER SEVENTEEN

"OK, gentlemen! Get your quarters ready!" McIver was full steam ahead as he started his instructions for firing the TOWs. Hallmark sat next to Vestal in the back of the classroom.

A slide series began to flash on the wall, and McIver pointed and talked as the slides changed, showing the technique and method for maximum accuracy. His delivery was good, and the students, with the exception of Sommerhill, seemed to be hanging with him.

Sommerhill would glance at the slides as they changed, then look back out the window. He nervously thumped the eraser of his pencil on the top of the desk, beating out his own bored rhythm. McIver noticed him, but continued on, undaunted by Sommerhill's seeming lack of interest.

The slides took forty-five minutes. As McIver finished, Hallmark signaled a fifteen-minute break. Sommerhill, seated near the door, bolted out of the room before McIver could reach him.

McIver watched him disappear and swung around to catch Hallmark's eye. The corporal's exit hadn't escaped Hallmark's attention. He nodded to McIver and left through the back door of the classroom.

Vestal remained seated as McIver walked over and sat down next to him.

"Good class, Sergeant McIver."

"Thanks, sir, but this blackboard-and-slide shit can't prove a thing till we have them behind the guns."

"You do your stuff in here, Mac, and I'll see to it that they get gun time." Vestal toyed with the paper in front of him. "By the way, I'm sorry I . . . really blew it for you guys."

McIver leaned back in the chair. "It don't really matter much to me, El-T. Some of the men had their hopes up, but they'll get over it."

"I tried to get transferred to another platoon."

"I know, sir. We heard, but I'm glad you didn't make it. This platoon works good together, we'll get past this."

Vestal looked up and smiled. "Thanks, Mac. I hope so."

McIver stood and picked up his notebook. "Just get us out to a training area, sir. The men don't mind the MREs and the sand when we're out there. They need to be busy; it's the best way to work all this out."

Hallmark reentered the room and called McIver back to the front desk.

"Did you catch up with him?" Mac asked, looking at Hallmark.

"Yeah. Seems he wants to file an EO complaint."

McIver wrinkled his face in disbelief. "What for?"

"He said there weren't any white guys out there

picking up cigarette butts and that it was done to humiliate him."

"Bullshit!" There weren't any other black guys out there either, and it was done because of his stupid Jody call this morning."

Hallmark nodded. "Yeah, I explained that to him, and he decided he wouldn't file the complaint, but he said he was through talking to me."

"Great! Are we going to lose him?" McIver asked. "I mean if he's going to tune us out, how am I going to get him to fire the TOW?"

Hallmark shrugged. "Let's give it some time, see how he tests in the classroom. If he screws up, I'll nail his hide to the wall."

"Yeah, and in the meantime who else have we got to train?"

"Sommerhill is a whole lot smarter than he acts sometimes. He'll come around. I wish that crazy woman he's married to would write him a decent letter. He's strung tight and this deal with the holiday leave has him overreacting."

The classroom filled as the break finished. Sommerhill came in just as the door was shutting.

Vestal stood and quietly left through the back door. He made his way down the hall to Captain Rodwell's office. If Rodwell was going to keep him, he decided, then he was going to let him do his job.

Training area availability was posted on the board in the OP's room. Area Bravo had a two-week opening; so did Romeo. The openings coincided with the end of McIver's training in the classroom.

Vestal's Virgins would be better off celebrating Christmas and New Year's at the training area than here at Champion Main. Coy set his jaw and walked into Rodwell's office.

CHAPTER EIGHTEEN

"Charges are set on ten-minute timers. Let's get the hell out of here!"

The two Kuwaiti freedom fighters and two American demolition experts ran down the alley as fast as they could and jumped into an old station wagon. The engine roared to life, and the car sped off down the narrow street. As they turned the corner into the urban neighborhood, the car slowed and two of the men jumped out. The car continued down the street slowly, then pulled up to the curb. The driver and his passenger stepped out, leaving the keys in the ignition, and walked briskly between two buildings. They were gone when the car exploded into a flaming fireball.

As the sound of the car explosion subsided, a new, larger explosion racked the area. People ran out into the street from their houses, screaming. An Iraqi jeep, loaded with heavily armed men, screeched to a stop near the flaming automobile. The men jumped out and ran toward the crowd of civilians gathered in the street. Soon the Iraqis were joined by an armored personnel carrier, full of soldiers, and two more jeeps, one armed with a fifty-caliber machine gun.

Two streets over, automatic weapons shattered what was left of the evening.

The first explosion was barely audible at the villa Tariq Shadi now occupied. Shadi wouldn't have paid too much attention to the second explosion either, except that immediately following the loud boom, the television screen went blank.

He grabbed the phone next to him. It was dead. He stared at the receiver in disgust and hurled the instrument into the wall. "Bareem!" he called out, and listened as the man hurried into the room.

"Sir!" Bareem panted.

"What is going on? We have no phones, no television! Are we under attack?" Shadi, who had been resting on the couch, hurriedly buttoned his tunic.

"I don't think so, sir," Bareem, bewildered, answered back.

Before Shadi could speak, another explosion, nearer this time, rattled the panes in the villa. Bareem and Shadi both hit the floor and covered their heads.

"I think it's the Kuwaitis again, sir," Bareem shouted across the room. The lights in the villa went out, and the two men were joined by several of Shadi's guards.

"Get out there and find out what's going on. Hurry! And send Captain Akkara over here with his infantry company, in case we are under attack. Get the field radios going!"

Bareem started out the door and staggered as

another explosion, this time only a block away, shook the ground. He regained control and fled out the door, toward Akkara's billets.

In groups of two, the Kuwaiti partisans slowly wound their way through darkened alleys and entered the burned-out shell of a building. They silently signaled their arrival to each other, then took positions along the walls and watched as others filed past in the darkness. Their leader, one of the Fazid brothers, knelt beside the Special Forces sergeant, and they counted as the people came in. Eight so far, and they had sent out ten men. They continued to wait a few minutes more, but nothing moved outside the building.

"That's it," the American said. "Let's see who's missing."

He and Fazid moved quietly from man to man, keeping conversation to a minimum. As they stepped over a broken stone wall, a figure wobbled toward them from the shadows of a nearby building, stumbled and fell forward. Fazid quickly ran from cover and knelt down by the man.

"It's Nabid!" he said, as the team sergeant zigzagged across the street to him.

They both knelt over the man.

"Go," the wounded man gasped. "I'm hit bad. The medic, the American, he's dead. They shot him before we could get back to . . ." He took one last breath as his body shuddered.

"He's gone," the sergeant said to Fazid. He could

feel no pulse. "Come on. We've got to get out of here."

The warehouse location was no longer safe. The partisans and Americans scattered and worked their way back into the city to their second safe house.

They had lost two men, a Kuwaiti and the American surgeon, but the mission had been a success. The television receiving tower and electricity plant were out. Phone lines were down, permanently shut off to the major section of the city. One of the Iraqi arsenals was still burning out of control.

As dawn broke over Kuwait City, the Iraqi commander met with his people to assess the damage. Colonel Shadi had not slept, and his eyes burned with the smoke from the burning arsenal nearby. Three of his tanks has been destroyed when the arsenal exploded. Although there hadn't been time for an inventory on the other vehicles, he knew there were more missing and destroyed.

Several companies of reinforcements had reached Kuwait City from Baghdad just as the explosions began. Their commander, Colonel Khalid, not a member of the Republican Guard, sat next to Shadi, all but ignored by the elite Guardsmen. It was no secret that many of Khalid's men had deserted during the night as explosions rocked the city.

Shadi listened as an engineer major described the damage to the electric power station.

127

"I feel sure," the major concluded, "that we will be able to have the damage repaired and all systems operating within three to four weeks, barring any further sabotage."

"Three to four weeks?" Shadi repeated.

"I'm afraid so, sir. Whoever blew this up knew exactly where to place the charges to do maximum damage. I'll have to send to Baghdad for replacement and people—"

"Enough from you," Shadi interrupted. "Just fix it!"

Bareem cleared his throat. "Sir, I find it difficult to believe the Kuwaitis operate on their own. Pieces of American explosives were found near the television tower. Reports are foreign terrorists help and supply the traitors."

"American, traitors," Shadi snarled down the length of the table. "Why has this happened? Where were our patrols, our guards?"

No one spoke around the table. Shadi slowly rose and shoved his chair back. "I'm going to report to Baghdad and get more instructions."

Bareem stood and gathered his notes. "I suppose, with the work to be done today, we should cancel the excecutions?"

"No! I don't want them canceled! Continue!" Shadi opened the door and left the room, without a word to the other commander.

Bareem sighed and sat back down in his chair. The engineer major leaned over to him. "Where are you going to put the bodies? The trench we dug for you last week is full."

"Then dig another one! You heard him. He wants the executions to continue." Bareem looked back at the man. "My job isn't easy either. Each day it becomes more difficult to find enough people to fill his execution quota."

The newly arrived commander looked down at Bareem. "Evidently they don't hide all the time. They certainly weren't hiding last night."

"Those are the one's I'd like to catch," Bareem said. "But it's as if they are ghosts."

Later, when Bareem joined Shadi at the villa, the commander was in a much better mood. "We're leaving. Colonel Gallenz will stay behind with part of his regiment to protect the airfield, and the new troops from Baghdad will take our places here."

Bareem was also pleased to be leaving Kuwait City. "Where are we going? Back to Baghdad?" he asked hopefully.

"No. We'll occupy our new bunkers and continue to fortify our position," Shadi said.

Conventional warfare, direct confrontation in the sand, with marked battle lines, was easy for Shadi. This unconventional fighting, the guerrilla warfare of the Kuwaiti nationals, made him uneasy. It was like swatting at a swarm of mosquitoes, exhausting and never ending, with no visible results.

"When do we leave?" Bareem asked.

"As soon as we gather our men and equipment. Take all the food you can find and as much water as possible," Shadi answered, busily packing his maps into a briefcase.

"*All* the food? What about the new troops? It could be a long time before supplies come in from Baghdad."

Shadi looked up, his face flushed bright red. "The replacements are not members of the Republican Guard. They are rejects and misfits, mere pieces and rags of the regular army. They will not be the ones to fight the great battle. We will! Their commander will see to their needs. I will see to mine."

CHAPTER NINETEEN

"Lieutenant Vestal, I've done it. All mail you requested is in there. Now get it out of here before someone finds out." The harassed clerk pointed to two large sand-colored bags lying on the ground.

"Thanks," Vestal said, grabbing up one of the bags and throwing it into his waiting HMMWV. The clerk just waved at him and hurried back into the warehouse. Neuhaus jumped out of the vehicle and helped Vestal with the last bag.

"How the hell did you do that, sir?" he asked as they shoved the bags to the back and got in to leave.

"You don't need to know." Vestal laughed, closing the door. "But don't let anyone know I was involved. Drop the first bag over at Laliker's unit, then bring this one over to my billet. We'll get it sorted and take it with us to the training area."

Neuhaus smiled. "Yes, sir. I think the guys should know you did this, though."

"No!"

"OK, sir, but it would certainly help your popularity with the men."

"You promised, Neuhaus," Vestal said. "Don't let me down."

Jeep Laliker and his men were standing outside the billets as Neuhaus drove up and unloaded the sack. SFC. Walker helped Neuhaus pull the bag from the HMMWV and waved as Neuhaus pulled away.

"What's that?" Jeep asked, looking at the bag.

"Mail, sir," Walker said, pulling the sack open. "Lots of mail and packages."

"Why are Vestal's people delivering our mail?" Laliker enquired curiously.

Walker scratched his head. "I don't know, come to think of it. Maybe because we're leaving today for ARAMCO. It must have been dropped over at the head shed, and they just sent it with Vestal's driver."

"Nice." Jeep raised his eyebrows, wrinkling his face into a smile. "Open her up, First Sergeant. Let's see what we got."

Two members of the platoon stepped up to help Walker distribute the mail. Within a few minutes the bag was empty. The scouts, letters and packages in hand, went inside to enjoy the long-awaited news and goodies from home. Their hosts from ARAMCO had arranged to pick them up after lunch in a double-decker bus at the gate, so the men hurried with their mail and finished packing. It was beginning to look a lot like Christmas.

"Sergeant Hallmark!" Vestal called out, walking toward the HMMWV where Hallmark and Neuhaus stood waiting. "Move 'em out! We're on our way to Bravo training area!"

132

The double-decker bus from ARAMCO stood at the gate as the TOW vehicles pulled by on their way to the training area. Hallmark spotted SFC. Walker and signaled for Neuhaus to stop. He jumped out and talked to the scout sergeant. Walker nodded and Hallmark patted him on the back, hurriedly shoving a piece of paper into his hand.

"No problem!" Walker shouted as the first sergeant turned to leave.

Hallmark waved over his shoulder, jumped back into the HMMWV and told Neuhaus to drive on.

"What was that all about?" Neuhaus asked.

"Just a little sergeant-to-sergeant business. Let's go."

The drive out to the training area took about three-and-a-half hours. As they drove along, a strong sandstorm, a *shamaal,* began to blow from the north. Powerful gusts of wind stirred the sand, obliterating the road ahead in places. As sturdy as the HMMWV was, the troops inside could still feel the wind buffeting them as they continued on.

McIver sat inside next to Sommerhill. He had his laptop on and was trying to get Eustas to pay attention to the diagram on the screen. "Are you listening to me?" he said, exasperated with the corporal's inattention.

"Yeah," Sommerhill said, blinking his eyes and yawning. "I hear you."

McIver, still not satisfied that he did, continued on. "Once you fire, you can be targeted, so we get the hell out, fall back to our concealed position, and the next team shoots." He moved the dots around on the screen. "See, like this."

Sommerhill glanced down. "Yeah . . . you've said that before, Sarge. I understand, OK?"

"Well, then act like it." McIver glowered at the corporal. "You're the one up on the guns. You better listen up."

"I told you, I'm *listening*."

"Sommerhill, this is serious shit. I have an assault and firing programmed into this computer. I want you to do it. It's just a game here, but it will teach you some of the principles. Here!" He shoved the computer into the corporal's hands.

After three completed sessions on the computer, Sommerhill had not only missed his targets, but he'd taken direct hits from the enemy tank. McIver snatched the computer away from him and shut it off. "Tomorrow, *on the sand,* I'm going to work your ass off." He slammed the computer shut.

Sommerhill watched as McIver folded his arms against his chest and leaned back against the side of the vehicle.

"So, big damn deal," he groaned. "I don't know how to work your stupid computer game. That don't mean I ain't gonna know how to fire the TOWs. I passed all your tests back at Main, didn't I?"

McIver just grunted.

"I did. I passed those suckers, and I can do this job." Sommerhill scowled. "You ain't gonna keep me driving these damn HMMWVs and picking up cigarette butts till my hitch is over, no siree."

"Watch it," McIver said calmly. "Just watch your mouth. Whatever happens to you is your decision."

"What does that mean?" Sommerhill asked angrily.

"Just that if you don't put some personal effort into it, you'll be a flunky for the rest of your life. You act stupid, you get treated like you're stupid."

Sommerhill sat still, glaring at the computer case next to McIver's feet. After a few minutes he reached over and picked it up. Placing it on his lap, he turned around to McIver. "How do you turn this thing on?"

Mac smiled and sat up, reaching over to open the case. "OK, now," he said, as the screen lit up, "just hit that key."

The game commenced. Although Sommerhill missed two of his six targets in the first round, he didn't get hit by the enemy, and he won the game on the next firing. He was getting into it. "OK, Mac! Set 'em up again," he said, pleased with his attempt. "I think I'm beginning to enjoy this."

Finally McIver had found a player for his game. "There's more to it than this," he warned, setting the screen up for a more difficult second game. "After we finish this round, I'll show you some tricks I've found to get a better lock on the target."

Genuine enthusiasm showed on Sommerhill's face as the second game began. He played well, listening as McIver helped him work through the intricacies of the game.

McIver found working with him, for the first

time, a real pleasure. The game, as close a simulation as McIver could get to a real situation, left
room for independent thinking. He was pleased as
he watched Sommerhill make decisions and figure
his way out of dangerous positions. Maybe, McIver
thought, watching Eustas blast along on the screen,
Sommerhill would make a good gunner.

The sandstorm was in full blow by the time they
arrived at Bravo. Hallmark hurried the men into
their tents and battened down for the heavy winds.
It was useless to try to get anything out of them
today. Lieutenant Vestal agreed to postpone any
work until morning.

The only thing Vestal insisted must be done was
the distribution of the mail. Hallmark was still
puzzled as to how Neuhaus had come by the bag of
letters and packages, all neatly sorted and bundled
for each man, but it was a blessing that didn't
require close scrutiny.

He threw the bag over his shoulder and trudged
out into the wind, to Sommerhill and Neuhaus's
tent. "Ho, ho, ho," he called and laughed as he
entered the tent and closed the flap. "It's Sergeant
Santa Claus!"

Neuhaus was lying on his cot, and Sommerhill
was still working with McIver's computer.

"Well," Hallmark said, still playing, "have you
been good little boys?" He reached down and pulled
out a package and tossed it to Neuhaus.

"What's this?" Neuhaus said. "I didn't get any
mail." He looked down at the parcel in his hands.
There was no postmark and no return address. It

was simply marked, "PFC. Michael Neuhaus." He tore open the wrapping and found two books inside, one a history of the 82nd Airborne and the other a book of poetry by Omar Khayyám.

"Who's this from?" Neuhaus asked as he looked up, smiling.

Hallmark just shrugged his shoulders and reached down into the pack again. "Who knows? Maybe there is a Santa Claus. And here's some mail for you, Sommerhill, but it looks like this just barely made it." He flipped the letters over to Eustas and then yanked out a bent-up tin box with a yellow Post-it note attached to the top. "Yep. 'Corporal Eustas Sommerhill.'" He pointed to the Magic Marker scribbling on the Post-it. "The wrapping must have been damaged so bad they had to relabel it at Dhahran." He handed the tin to Sommerhill.

Eustas looked at the yellow paper. "Yeah, that's me, but who sent it?"

"Probably from Kisha. It smells like cookies," Hallmark said, smiling.

"Hot damn!" Sommerhill yanked the top off the tin and pulled back the tissue paper. "It *is* cookies. Chocolate-chip cookies!" He took one and passed the tin over to Neuhaus. "That's funny, 'cause there ain't a letter from her in here . . . Just two from my momma and some more of that Black Panther shit!"

Neuhaus took a cookie and handed one to Hallmark before returning the tin to Sommerhill. Hallmark took a bite, then grabbed the sack and threw it over his shoulder. "Mmmm, these are good! You

137

tell Kisha thanks from me. I gotta go now. Santa has to make his rounds, you know!" He laughed again as he opened the tent flap and disappeared into the swirling sand.

"This is really weird," Sommerhill said, stuffing another cookie into his mouth. "I mean, I ain't questioning it, but Kisha is a shitty cook. These are really great cookies. I didn't know she knew how to bake . . . I guess somebody at the support group, or whatever that is she's doing, helped her."

Neuhaus stole a quick look at his tentmate, then eased back on his cot. He knew where those cookies had come from, and it wasn't Kisha Sommerhill. But the books were another matter. He'd sorted the mail with Lieutenant Vestal. When they repacked, there hadn't been anything for him.

"Hey, sir," Hallmark yelled outside the tent. "It's me."

"Come on in." Vestal put down his notebook and opened the tent flap for him. "Mail distributed?"

"Yes, sir. It's gonna be a better Christmas than I thought. I still can't figure how Neuhaus got that out to us. There wasn't any on the last supply train at Main."

Vestal pulled out an extra camp stool and motioned for Hallmark to sit. "I don't know . . . Maybe someone made a run into Dhahran or something. Everybody settled in and ready to train tomorrow?" He sat down.

"Yeah." Hallmark reached up and rubbed the

sand out of his eyes. "Of course, we'll need to clean everything, providing this wind permits us to."

"It will. I talked to one of the artillery officers a few minutes ago. He said this is supposed to die down tonight and clear tomorrow."

"Good! I'm glad you were able to get us out here. I understand it was a hell of a battle convincing Rodwell."

"Oh yeah?" Coy cocked his head, smiling. "And where did you hear that?"

"Battalion sergeant major said he was over there when you were pressing your case. Said the building shook while you two argued."

Vestal grinned. "It wasn't that bad."

Hallmark rose and started to leave. "Well, I'm glad you won. The men needed this. Having them out here, away from Main, and mail on top of it, why, it's going to make my job a whole lot easier. Their morale should be at peak level by tomorrow."

Vestal stood and loosened the tent flap. "Good. Merry Christmas, Van." He held out his hand.

"Merry Christmas to you!" Hallmark shook his hand. "Funny," he added. "Everyone got something but you this time. Well, see you later."

Vestal fastened the tent flap behind Hallmark and sat down on his cot. He lifted his notebook back onto his lap and continued writing where he had left off. "The cookies were great, Mom. My favorite, chocolate chip. You never forget. By the way, tell Uncle Don and Aunt Clara thanks for the books. I'll try to get them a letter off later. Wouldn't you know, he sent me *The History of the 82nd Airborne*.

You tell him, I'm making history! Aunt Clara, always the scholar, sent me some of Omar Khayyám's poetry. Pretty neat, reading that stuff in the place where it was written. Well, I gotta turn in now. Don't worry and remember I love you. Coy." Vestal tore out the paper and stuffed it into an envelope, then lay back down on his cot.

CHAPTER TWENTY

"Helluva sandstorm, ain't it, Lieutenant Laliker?" The oilman from ARAMCO shouted above the wind as he helped load Laliker's gear on the bus.

"Yes, sir. It is that." Jeep stepped on board and swung into the vacant front seat. The oilman got in and sat down beside him. He held out his hand. "Hi, I'm Al Cunningham. Glad to have you with us!"

Laliker shook his hand. "Please, call me Jeep, and I can't tell you how glad we are to be with you, Mr. Cunningham."

"Al!" the man corrected him. "Just Al. Tell me, how'd you get a name like Jeep?"

"My initials—G.P.," Laliker answered. "My folks started calling me Jeep, and it stuck."

"Sounds good to me." Cunningham reached down to pull up a thermos bottle, unscrewed the lid and poured a drink.

"Here." He offered the cup to Laliker. "Fresh lemonade with ice. I'm only sorry I can't offer you a beer."

Jeep took the cup and sipped. "Mmm, that's good. Thanks." Al Cunningham nodded, pulling an extra cup from under the seat for himself. He filled it and screwed the thermos lid back on carefully.

He was a big, friendly man, about six-two, two hundred pounds, with a few strands of gray blending with his brown hair at the temples. Laliker figured he was in his late forties.

"Where are you from in the States?" Cunningham asked.

"Texas. A town called Marfa, down in the Big Bend."

"No kidding. I'm from San Antonio. My daughter is a senior at the university in Austin."

"Oh yeah? I graduated from Texas A&M."

"An Aggie! That's great. Listen," Cunningham said, pulling a sheet of paper from his pocket, "I wish you'd check this over for me. I asked your Captain Rodwell, when we made the arrangements to pick you up, for all the names of your people." He handed the list to Jeep. "Is this correct?"

Jeep looked down at the list. "Yes, sir. I see your name next to mine. What does that mean?" he asked, handing the list back to Cunningham.

"I wrote down the names of who would be staying with each family. You'll be staying at our home."

"Listen, sir, I mean Al, this is just great what you're doing here, having us out and all. We really appreciate it."

Cunningham shook his head. "Oh, no. It's our privilege and pleasure to have you people as our guests. My wife is afraid, with all the crap going on, that our daughter won't make it in for the holidays. You'll be welcome comfort if that happens. She's in Riyahd right now, at the airport, and I hope Maggie made the plane."

142

"Maggie?"

"That's our daughter. We routed her through Athens, so she may make it in."

Jeep smiled and looked out the window. Great, he thought to himself, I'm being set up to entertain their daughter.

"Say! Do you like to swim?" Cunningham asked, as Jeep turned back to face him. "We're right on the Persian Gulf, beautiful sandy beach. Of course, the water is awfully salt. But does it ever make you buoyant. You couldn't sink out there if you wanted to!"

Jeep wondered, listening to the man as he talked on about swimming and boating, what his daughter looked like. He imagined himself lounging on the beach with a politically correct, 250-pound tea sipper from U.T. Austin.

Al Cunningham was still listing all the amenities as the ARAMCO compound came into view. At first Jeep thought they were coming to a large town; then he saw the sign and the fence around the perimeter.

The compound was where the employees and families of the company lived and worked, including the company headquarters and a large processing plant. The oil was pumped in, via the pipelines, and converted for shipping right there on the property.

The bus slowed down and stopped. One of the gate guards, a Saudi armed with an automatic rifle, gave the driver permission to enter a large parking lot. There were fifty or more golf carts parked in front of the headquarters.

"Well, this is as far as the bus goes. Now we ride in our only mode of transport on the compound—golf carts!" Cunningham said as they stepped outside.

There were several families waiting near the carts as the soldiers stepped from the bus. They moved forward, calling out names and gathering up their designated houseguests. Jeep stared as they walked up and hugged his men, welcoming them. Some of the ARAMCO people even had banners, each with a soldier's name on it. Jeep felt his eyes fill, just watching. Several of his men had tears running down their cheeks as they accepted the warm welcome from their hosts and hostesses.

"By God," Jeep said out loud, "we may not be home, but this is as close as it gets!"

Cunningham smiled and patted him on the back. "Come on, Jeep, you drive." He motioned toward the golf cart with "Al's Camel" painted on the fender.

Jeep turned and tossed his gear in the back. "Yes, sir! Just point the way."

"Straight down this street, past the movie house and the church, then turn right at the commissary. Your home for the next seven days is the third house from the corner," Cunningham said, as they pulled out of the parking lot. "Let's hurry. I think my wife said she'd left some ham-and-cheese sandwiches for us."

144

"Ham!" Jeep exclaimed. "How fast does this thing go?" They both laughed as the golf cart zoomed down the street. Jeep was relaxing; this could be all right.

As they pulled into the drive, Jeep whistled. "Wow, this looks just like the States. And on the beach," he said, looking around. "It's fantastic."

Al grabbed his gear before Jeep could stop him and carried it up to the front porch. The smell of fresh pine filled the air as they opened the door. A large, beautifully decorated tree stood in the entryway, its tiny lights twinkling on thick limbs. Jeep stepped back. "I don't believe this. I haven't seen a real tree in ages. My mom's into easy storage."

Cunningham stepped past him and into the hall. "Come on, I'll show you your room." Jeep followed him to a door that opened on a medium-sized room with a double bed. Sliding glass doors fronted a patio and the beach beyond. The room was bright sunshine yellow, with large jungle-patterned drapes and bedspread. A private bathroom adjoined the bedroom. Bananas and apples, artfully arranged in a bowl, sat next to the bed on the nightstand.

Laliker was awed.

"I don't know how to thank you," he said, tears welling up in his eyes. Embarrassed, he turned his head. "I'm sorry, it's just been such a long time. I forgot what it was like to be in a home, around a family."

Al looked away. "It's OK. I'm glad you're here. You can freshen up in the bathroom and meet me

145

back in the kitchen." He closed the door and left Jeep with his privacy.

The kitchen was big and friendly, with doors that opened onto a side patio with a barbecue pit. Cunningham had his sandwich and was eating it at an oval-shaped table when Laliker joined him. All the fixings were laid out on the sideboard. Al motioned for him to help himself.

As he piled on the ham, Jeep noticed a large plaque hanging on the sideboard. "Let's see," he said. "My Spanish is a little rusty, but that says 'My Home is Your Home,' right?"

"That's right. Good, you speak Spanish. My wife will love that. She's from Barcelona." Cunningham took another bite.

Jeep finished making his sandwich and sat down next to Al. "I try, but I'm afraid mine is more Tex-Mex than real Spanish."

"She'll love you anyway. She likes tall, good-looking Texans. She married me, didn't she?"

Jeep laughed. "When will your wife get back?" he asked, taking a bite from his sandwich.

"Anytime now. She's flying in on the company plane. If Maggie made it, she would have landed about an hour and a half ago. It's about a forty-five-minute flight from Riyadh. Finish up and we'll go get you some civilian clothes from next door. My neighbor's about your size. You'll be more comfortable out of those BDUs."

"That would work," Jeep said, smiling.

The neighbor was his size, and after visiting for

a few minutes, they returned to the house with several pairs of shorts and shirts. Jeep stepped into his room and emerged to join Al for a walk on the beach in a pair of tan shorts, a wild Hawaiian shirt and his shower shoes.

He had never seen so many shells lying on a beach before. They were everywhere—starfish, sand dollars and near-perfect conchs. As they walked along, he and Al discussed Hussein and the invasion of Kuwait. Several of the Cunninghams' friends who worked for ARAMCO had escaped in the first month after the invasion. Al retold some of their grim observations of the Iraqi conquerors.

"The Iraqis are real bastards," Cunningham said. "They aren't going to leave until they strip everything out of Kuwait. They are murdering, looting and raping that country."

Jeep nodded in agreement. "I've never seen that much damage done to a human being," he said, referring to the refugees he'd found near Romeo training area.

Someone called out Cunningham's name from the houses behind them. They both turned and watched as two women hurried along the sand. "It's Madelena and Maggie," Cunningham said, dragging Jeep along. "She made it!"

As they drew nearer, Jeep quickened his step. The two women looked like sisters, both tall blondes with strikingly angular faces. Cunningham broke into a run and grabbed the younger of the two women, crushing her in a bear hug.

147

As they greeted one another, Jeep stood back, looking at the Cunningham women. He had heard of the beautiful blondes in Spain, descendants of the northern invaders centuries ago, but he'd never seen one before. Madelena was definitely a prime example, and Maggie, who now flashed her blue-green eyes at him, was nothing short of incredible.

She broke away from her father's grasp and faced Jeep. "And you must be Lieutenant Laliker, our guest for Christmas," she said, holding out her hand. "We're glad to have you with us."

"Call him Jeep!" her father called out over her shoulder.

"Hi! And thanks for having me." Jeep shook her hand and turned, finding it hard to break away from Maggie's intense eyes, to meet her mother.

Madelena Cunningham was as gracious and warm as her husband. She embraced Jeep, welcoming him to their home. The greeting done, Al walked with Madelena back to the house, leaving Jeep and Maggie together on the beach.

"Let's walk," she said, reaching down to take off her shoes. "You can tell me all about yourself."

Jeep reached over and held her arm while she loosened the straps on her sandals. "Well, there's not really that much to tell," he said, watching her hair as the sun played on it. But talk he did, surprised at how quickly he warmed to her. They walked to the end of the fenced perimeter, about a mile down the beach, then turned and walked back into the compound's little picnic area.

148

A cluster of palm trees provided shade over one of the tables, and they sat down, as Jeep, embarrassed but unable to stop, continued to pour out his life story.

It wasn't just her beauty that held him captive; there was something else, something he'd never experienced before. She was open and honest, filled with curiosity, intelligent and witty. Within the first hour, he felt as if he'd known her all his life.

Bob Walker excused himself from his ARAMCO family and went over to use the phone they'd offered him. He pulled from his pocket the piece of paper Hallmark had given him and dialed the number. Within a few minutes the connection was made.

"Yes," he said into the receiver, "this is an overseas call from Saudi Arabia. I'd like to speak to Mr. Michael Neuhaus the third, please." He waited while the secretary connected them. "Yes, Mr. Neuhaus? You have a fax machine in your office, sir?" he asked the voice on the line. "Good . . . No, it doesn't matter who I am. I want you to take down this information. It will give you a way to communicate with your son. He needs to hear from you."

Jeep stood in the shower, deep in thought as the warm water rushed over him. He could hardly wait to finish and get back to her. Confused feelings ran over him like the warm water. He wanted to be with her, just near her, just to listen to her laughter or watch her face as she changed expressions. She wasn't like any woman he'd ever met before, yet a composite of all of them. Physically, he wanted her, but he felt that if he touched her, it would somehow break the magic between them. He turned off the faucet and reached for a towel.

Sitting on the edge of the bed, he thought about his visit with Colley. She was exciting, and certainly knew her way around men, but he'd never been able to talk to her. Their relationship, if that's what it could be called, was purely physical. She was shallow and self-centered. He came to the quick realization that he didn't care if he ever saw her again.

Hurriedly he yanked on another of the neighbor's shirts and a pair of shorts and joined the Cunninghams out by the barbecue grill. Maggie met him at the patio door and beamed as he neared her. This, he thought to himself, gazing into her smiling face, is the best Christmas of my life.

The rest of the scout platoon, now settled into their guest homes, were being treated royally. The families had all prepared well for them, including an individual present under each tree with the visiting platoon member's name on it.

The hospitality of the ARAMCO people was well known by all the troops who'd had the pleasure of being their guests previously, but the scouts felt the praise had been understated. Unlimited long-distance calls, with the cost absorbed by ARAMCO, made it possible for everyone to call his own family back in the States. It was one of those miracles of human kindness found in a war zone.

Jeep knew, sitting at the table with the Cunninghams, as they all did, that this week would pass much too quickly.

CHAPTER TWENTY-ONE

Sommerhill was smokin'. Two weeks of intensive training with live ammunition had proven his ability on the missile system. The reluctant apprentice was now master of the game. McIver was as proud of him as he was of himself.

"Did you see that?" Mac nudged the man next to him. "He's hot!"

Hallmark watched as the blown target in the distance continued to flame. "He is that."

"Hell," McIver said, adjusting his glasses, "and in the MOPP headgear, no less! I tell you, Eustas is one red-hot gunner, even better than I am."

Having fired their last round, the HMMWV turned and thundered back to the rear, where the two sergeants were waiting. Sommerhill shimmied out of the firing turret, slid to the ground and yanked off the heavy headgear. He was wet with sweat, but smiling from ear to ear. Neuhaus ran excitedly from the driver's side and gave Sommerhill a high five.

"OK!" Neuhaus yelled. "You 'killed' 'em all!"

"That was some fancy driving you did out there, too. It put me in position for some good shots. Thanks," Sommerhill said, throwing his arm over

Neuhaus's shoulder as they joined Hallmark and McIver.

Vestal sat with the second HMMWV crew and watched as they all patted one another on the back, elated with the accomplishments of the last two weeks. He reached over and signaled his driver to take him back to the encampment. It was time to go back to Main now, and this time he didn't dread it. Holidays in his past had been more comfortable, more fun, but he'd never spent one more productive or satisfying. This New Year's Eve was one to celebrate.

Jeep Laliker stood in line and waited. He held out a long-distance calling card to the AT&T official as he stepped forward, next to use their portable phone setup.

The man smiled and shook his head. "Just reverse the charges," he said, and handed Laliker a clipboard to sign. "Where you callin', son?"

"It's local. I have a number in the ARAMCO compound," Jeep responded, quickly signing his name as the man ahead of him hung up.

"Hell," the AT&T man laughed, accepting the board back, "don't worry about charges. Just dial the number! Happy New Year, Lieutenant!"

Jeep nodded and picked up the receiver, rapidly punching out the number on the lighted panel. He listened as the phone rang, then rang again . . . and again. He was about to hang up when the receiver clicked.

"Hello?"

A warm rush covered him as he heard her voice. "Maggie! It's me," he said, closing his eyes and conjuring an image of her in his mind.

"Jeep!" she exclaimed. "God, I was hoping it would be you!"

"I just called to wish you and your folks a happy New Year. How are you?" he asked.

"We're great, but we all miss you."

Jeep held the receiver tightly. "Listen, I don't have much time, but tell everyone thanks again for me. The guys had a great time."

"We did, too." There was a long pause.

He felt stupid. There were so many things he wanted to say to her, but the sound of her voice seemed to have struck him dumb. "Uh . . . when are you returning to the States? I mean, aren't you supposed to leave soon for spring semester?"

"Yes, I leave on the sixteenth of January. Why? Do you think you'll be able to get back out here?"

He heard the hope in her voice. "No," he answered, "I just want you to get back . . . safely, that is. I have a feeling things are about to pop."

"I know, I do, too . . . Jeep?" She paused.

"Yes," he answered anxiously.

"I miss you. I don't want to leave now. I . . ." Her voice broke. He heard her crying.

"Don't, Maggie, don't cry. I'll be all right. I promise you. You and I have a lot to talk over when this is through. I'm going to find you." He felt a tightness in his chest and knew if he continued, he would break, too. "I've got to go now. Stay safe and wait for me, Maggie. I need you."

154

• • •

Vestal's Virgins were the conversation over lunch in the headquarters at Main. Captain Rodwell, gratified with his men's work, listened to the comments from other company commanders that had just returned from the training area.

"Looks like your errant lieutenant got his shit together," one of the captains commented. "His new gunner is kicking ass out there."

"Sure! They're Delta Company, aren't they?" Rodwell said with pride.

He was aware of the work Vestal had done to correct his mistake. It was a smart move to get them to the training area, but that was something he wouldn't have suggested or offered the lieutenant. It had to be a decision Vestal came to by himself.

They had fought the day he stormed into Rodwell's office demanding the two weeks at Romeo. Rodwell wanted Vestal to fight for his men. He'd done it, and the Virgins were united again.

Laliker and his scout platoon had returned from their R&R rested and in high spirits. All in all, Rodwell thought to himself, the Company was in good shape. And it was a good thing, because tomorrow was the fifteen of January, the deadline set for Hussein to withdraw from Kuwait. There was no indication that he intended to do so.

The supply train pulled into Main and stopped as Hallmark and McIver waited.

"Any mail?" McIver shouted over to the driver.

"Not really, just one fax," the driver said, wiping sweat from his eyes. "The mail has been halted until we get all these supplies out to the field."

"Figures! We haven't had any mail since Christmas. Who's the fax for?" Hallmark asked.

"Uhh, let's see . . . PFC. Michael Neuhaus IV . . . Delta Company . . ."

"He's one of mine," Hallmark said, interrupting him. "I'll take it."

The driver reached out the window and handed the paper to Hallmark. McIver stared at the message in his hand. "Neuhaus? Who's writing Neuhaus? He hasn't gotten a letter since we've been over here."

"I don't know, but I think I saw him earlier in the dayroom," Hallmark said, stubbing out his cigarette and slipping the butt in his pocket. "I'll meet you in the weight room in a few minutes, Mac. Let me run this on over to Neuhaus."

Hallmark found him shooting pool with one of Laliker's scouts. He handed him the envelope and left without commenting. Curious, but unwilling to let anyone see him read the letter, Neuhaus put it in his pocket and walked out of the building.

He had no idea who would send him a fax, no idea who would even write him. He walked over and sat down on one of the bleachers by the soccer field.

Taking a deep breath, he took the message out and started to read.

"Dear Michael, I know we've had some angry words. I've got something to tell you, not that it excuses what I've done, but it at least gives a reason. Twenty-five years ago, I did something I am still ashamed of. I never told you, but I fought the draft and got an exemption, to avoid going to Vietnam. When you announced your enlistment into the service and your withdrawal from Harvard, the reverse of what I did, I was angry. Not with you, but with myself. You had the guts I never had, so to avoid facing my own cowardice, I disowned you. Having you around, hearing your name, would only underline the disgust I feel for what I did. Since you've been gone, I have been stubbornly holding my line. Secretly, however, perhaps from my better nature, if creatures such as I have one, I prayed you were somewhere in the States, safely pushing paper back and forth on an Army desk. Today, a friend of your Sergeant Hallmark called me, and my illusion has been shattered. You are there, in harm's way, doing what I should have done twenty-five years ago. I love you, son. Come home safe and sound. Your father, Michael Fitzpatrick Neuhaus III."

He read the page over again, then folded it neatly and stuffed it back in his pocket. Courage, he thought to himself, is shown in many ways. He hadn't quit Harvard and joined the Army to fight. He surely hadn't imagined then that he would be sitting in Saudi Arabia today, waiting to fight a million-man tank army. Maybe he wouldn't have done it, if he'd known. He could only speculate, because he'd had no real decision to make. To be honest, he had to admit he'd done it because he was bored.

He got up and walked over to the AT&T portable message center. "How do you send a fax to the States?" he asked the man standing at the door of the van.

The man picked up a piece of paper and handed it to him. "Just fill this out and write your message underneath. It'll be there tomorrow."

"Thanks." Neuhaus leaned over the makeshift counter and wrote something down, looked it over and handed it back to the man.

"Hey." The man looked at the brief message. "You can send up to two pages."

"No," Neuhaus said, walking away, "that's enough."

"Well, OK. Happy New Year!"

"Yeah. Happy New Year to you, too!" Neuhaus called out over his shoulder.

The AT&T man looked down at the paper as the soldier left. Other than the address, all he'd written was "Thanks, Dad. Your son, No-Hero Michael."

Vestal was sitting in his room, catching up on some of his own correspondence, when the door opened. Irritated at the unannounced interruption, he looked up, ready to lash out at the intruder. Instead, as he saw Jeep Laliker standing there, he eased back in the chair.

"Hi. Come on in," he said, warily.

"Thanks," Jeep said, walking in and closing the door behind him. He had a sack in his hand.

"Listen . . . ," Vestal started.

"I don't want to hear it," Jeep interrupted. "Yesterday was yesterday. You paid, Coy, now it's over. I came over to bury the hatchet." He stripped the paper sack off a bottle.

"What is that? Champagne?" Vestal sat forward, staring in disbelief. "How in the hell did you manage that?"

Jeep laughed. "I wish it were champagne, but sparkling cider was the best the ARAMCO commissary could do!" He removed the foil and twisted the wire around the cork. "You got any glasses in here?"

Coy scrambled through some things at his feet and produced two empty cans. "Hey," he said, as Jeep eyed them with suspicion, "they're clean!"

Jeep took the cans, still not convinced, and wiped them out with the tail of his T-shirt. Carefully he filled them and offered one to Coy.

"OK," Vestal said, accepting, "what's the occasion?"

"The mail . . . Walker found out about your little trip into Dhahran. Thanks."

"No problem." Vestal looked down at the cup in his hands. "Figured I needed to mend some fences."

Jeep nodded. "Yep, but you didn't tell anyone you did it. How'd you figure to get credit?"

"Didn't do it to get credit."

Jeep stared at him. "No, that's what I figured. It made things nice for me and my guys, though."

Coy looked up from the can of cider. "Are we going to drink this stuff or bathe in it?"

"Well, we'll probably wish we'd bathed in it, but let's drink it. First a toast!"

"OK." Coy smiled, holding his cider up. "What to, the new year?"

"No." Jeep reached over and touched his drink to Vestal's. "How about to tomorrow?"

Vestal looked down at his watch. "Tomorrow is the fifteenth of January . . ." He smiled. "Good toast, Jeep! To tomorrow it is!"

They both took a sip. Jeep coughed and looked up. "God! This is awful! Let's wash our socks in it!"

"I'm glad you said that." Vestal laughed. "I thought you already had!"

Hallmark found Walker in the dayroom watching TV and sat down beside him. "Hey, how's the war going?" he asked, looking up at the screen.

"Media pukes winning by a mile!" Walker said, turning to face him. "Hussein hasn't moved an inch."

"That's what I heard. Oh well, should be interesting. If we're not out laying Iraqis down like wheat tomorrow, how'd you like to have a football game? My platoon against yours?"

"We'll be doing trench training tomorrow. On the sixteenth we have classroom until early afternoon, but yeah, I think the guys would like it, say about nineteen hundred, day after tomorrow?" Walker took out his notebook to write down the date.

"Yeah, that fits our schedule, too. By the way, thanks for handling that Neuhaus business for me," Hallmark said, rising to go.

"Sure. How'd it work out?" Walker asked.

"I think it's going to be fine," Hallmark said, strolling to the door. "Just fine."

Accustomed to being on alert, the men of the 82nd did nothing special on January 15. Nothing in the routine at Champion Main marked the significance of the date.

Vestal tried to phone Colley in Dhahran, only to be told that the MPs were moving to Riyadh.

CHAPTER TWENTY-TWO

At 0130 hours, January 17, 1991, allied planes from bases in Saudi Arabia and carriers in the Persian Gulf crossed the borders of Iraq and Kuwait. Coordination came from E-3A Sentry AWACs radar planes. The bombing would start at 0300 hours. In the initial wave about two dozen F-117A stealth fighter bombers took off, their mission to knock out Iraqi communications.

The main bomber wave of the first strike consisted of twenty-two US Air Force F-15E Strike Eagle fighter bombers, flying low to attack military targets, and a pair of EF-111 Ravens, which jammed the Iraqi radar. Navy and Marine A-6E Intruder attack bombers, joined by British Tornados and twenty Saudi F-15C fighters, provided escort and protection for the bombers.

Ground-hugging Tomahawk Cruise Missiles whipped off the decks of U.S. battleships in the Persian Gulf and joined the flying armada headed for Baghdad. Well planned and well executed, the bombing was over in thirty minutes. The shield was in place; now it was time for the storm.

McIver, unable to sleep, had gone down to the dayroom to watch TV. There were a couple of soldiers, just off guard duty, sprawled on the floor, sleepily gazing at the tube. Mac looked around for the coffeepot and poured himself a cup of the evil-smelling brew, then settled in a chair. CNN was running their usual speculation-versus-reality news and switching to their reporters in Baghdad as he took his first sip of coffee.

"Hey," one of the soldiers said, sitting up, "if CNN can go there, why can't we?"

The picture on the TV was of CNN's reporter, Bernard Shaw, looking out the window in Baghdad and explaining the heightened sense of alert, what the citizens of Baghdad had done that day and the euphoria of the Iraqis that the deadline had passed with no action from the U.S. or its allies. Suddenly he lurched closer to the window.

"Wait a minute," the newsman said. "What's that? It looks like a missile!" There was a loud blast on the streets below. "It *is* a missile! I'm going to move away from the window, now!"

The soldiers still lying on the floor sprang to seated positions, eyes glued to the TV. Mac leaned forward, spilling his coffee.

Shaw, joined by others in his room at Baghdad's Al Rashid Hotel, began to talk excitedly. "My God, we're under attack!" Iraqi air-raid sirens began to blare in the background, amid sounds of explosions. The newsman, obviously shaken, nervously looked from the window and said, "I knew I should have left here yesterday."

The men in the dayroom broke into laughter, and the realization seemed to hit them all at the same time. They danced around the room, hoo-ahing their excitement.

"It's started! Thank God, it's started!" McIver jumped from his chair and walked closer so he could hear. The scene from CNN's vantage point in Baghdad was one of total chaos. Bombs were blasting away and the broadcast was erratic.

The picture on the screen switched to the newsroom, where one of the network's anchor people tried to ask Shaw questions. Shaw gulped out his answers, fighting for his journalistic cool, but it was clear to everyone that something was happening in Baghdad.

The noise in the dayroom attracted attention, and others began to walk in, electrified by the news, which was now being shouted down the halls.

McIver spun around, tossing his cup on the floor, and sprang to the door, hurrying out to find Hallmark. He was almost out of breath as he threw open the sergeant's door.

"Hit the ground, Van!" he shouted into the darkened room. "The balloon is up! We're bombing the crap out of Baghdad!"

Hallmark jumped from his sleeping bag and yanked on his trousers. "Fan-fucking-tastic!" he exclaimed, as he joined McIver in the hallway.

Everyone around Hallmark's room heard McIver's news, and they, too, emerged into the hallway. Within thirty minutes there was standing-room only in the dayroom and the news was confirmed. The U.S. and its allies had struck a deafening first blow against Iraq.

The men and women at Champion Main went outside and gazed up at the sky to await the sound of the returning planes. If the energy of their excitement could have been harnessed that morning, it would have created a bomb more powerful than any yet devised. The long wait in the sand was now coming to an end. The soldiers of the 82nd Division didn't know what the days ahead would bring, but they knew it wouldn't be the anxious waiting they'd been enduring. The war had started, and the warriors were more than ready.

Sommerhill was last to join the platoon outside. He stood next to Neuhaus and rubbed his eyes sleepily. "What's happening?" he asked, suppressing a yawn.

"All hell's busted loose, Eustas. We're bombing Baghdad!"

Sommerhill looked up into the night sky as the first of the bombers returned overhead, their faraway rumble drowned out by the cheers from the assembled soldiers. "Well," he said, stretching his arms, "I guess we ain't gonna have no PT this morning."

As the men reentered the dayroom, President George Bush was on TV. His words, ringing out over the speakers, confirmed what they already knew. "The world could wait no longer," Bush said, ". . . The liberation of Kuwait is close at hand."

Neuhaus, McIver and Hallmark stood on the parade field next to Vestal, still watching as the sky began to lighten. There were jet trails mixed with light clouds as dawn came to the Middle East.

165

Suddenly they saw two fast-moving objects zinging southward over their heads. "What the hell . . . ?" Neuhaus said, watching the projectiles.

Abruptly loud whooshing noises filled the air as six jet streams flashed out overhead and intercepted the two incoming missiles, resulting in a fiery aerial explosion. The sky lit up like the Fourth of July, complete with high-altitude blasts resembling Roman candles.

"What the hell was that?" Neuhaus asked Vestal.

Vestal stared as the last of the light show in the sky subsided. "You're asking me? Shit, who do I look like, W.E.B. Griffith? I'm just a lieutenant, Neuhaus. I have, however, ruled out fast flying birds!"

"It was SCUDs coming from Iraq, I'll bet," McIver said. "We must have intercepted with Patriot Missiles."

"I been hearing about those 'SCUDs,'" Neuhaus said, looking at McIver. "I'm not clear on what they are, though."

"They're just big rockets," McIver responded. "Not at all reliable, extremely inaccurate. We unloaded some like them from our arsenals back in 1974 or '75. The last one the U.S. had was the 'Honest John Missile.' Thank God we went ahead and built the Patriot system."

"So," Neuhaus seemed to relax, "the SCUDs are harmless?"

"No, not if they manage to land on you, they're not! They're thirty-seven-feet long, truck-launched and capable of carrying one hell of a warhead. They

166

can be fitted with chemicals or gas. No," McIver shook his head, "I wouldn't call them harmless."

"So how do the Patriots get them?" Neuhaus asked.

Hallmark was impressed at Mac's knowledge of missiles. He lit a cigarette and listened as McIver explained the Air Defense Artillery's missile system.

"Radar identifies and tracks the incoming SCUD, then the Patriot fires and intercepts." Mac smiled, happy to share his knowledge.

"Then," Neuhaus concluded, "we don't have to worry about them."

"You need to keep on worrying, Neuhaus," McIver said, patting the PFC on the shoulder. "The Patriot only has a range of fifty miles or so. They're going to be popping those SCUDs right over our heads. If they miss, or get a bad hit, knocking the SCUD off its course, it could light up your life!"

As the day continued, McIver's speculation that the missiles fired from the north were SCUDS was confirmed. The Iraqis unleashed several more into Saudi Arabia and Israel. The attacks were preceded by loud air-raid sirens directing all personnel to don their MOPP gear and hurry to the nearest bomb shelter.

The incoming SCUDS did no damage in Saudi Arabia, but Israel was getting pounded. All involved held their breath, hoping that the aggressive little nation, well known for its immediate and bloody responses, could resist the urge to fight back. Within three days, Patriot Missile systems and U.S. crews were in Tel Aviv, setting up Israel's defense. The coalition, a near-impossible collection of Arabs, all of whom harbored a deep-seated hatred of Israel, was fragile at best. If Israel struck back against Iraq, as its citizens were demanding, the game could change overnight.

The atmosphere during the days of the air war was tense and expectant. As the sands began to swirl in January's normal windstorms, the ground troops, trained and ready for action, pulled themselves into position, either to defend or to go on the offensive. Saddam Hussein's words, "The great showdown has begun. The mother of all battles is under way," became an often used slogan among the troops as they prepared.

This was no longer a training exercise, no longer just a "show of force." Vestal and Hallmark knew, as they worked steadily with the men of the TOW platoon, that this was to be the ultimate EXEVAL, with heavy penalties for any misfires. Now, thought Hallmark as he oversaw the loading of the missiles onto their racks, the targets will be shooting back.

CHAPTER TWENTY-THREE

As the Division prepared to move, all communications to the civilian world ceased. Laliker spied a FAC officer walking away from Division Artillery headquarters and starting toward his waiting HM-MWV.

"Hey," Jeep shouted, running to the man. "You from Riyadh?"

"Yes," the man said and nodded as Jeep joined him.

"Did any civilian flights leave on January 16th?" he asked.

"I can't say for sure," the Air Force officer replied, "but it's doubtful. We had a few things to do that day, and it's unlikely they were able to get clearance."

"Can you still phone out, in-country, that is?"

The officer looked puzzled. "Yeah, I guess so. Why?"

Jeep yanked a page from his notebook and scribbled down Cunningham's number. "I need a favor. Please call these folks, and tell them I'll get in touch with them as soon as I can. Can you do that?"

"Depends," the man responded. "Where's this call going?"

169

"To a family out at the ARAMCO compound," Jeep said, handing him the paper. "I'd really appreciate it."

"No problem." The man slipped the note into his flight suit.

"Hey," Jeep said, watching the officer slide into the HMMWV. "You guys are doing great up there. Just keep pounding the shit out of them!"

"Don't worry, Lieutenant," the man said, as the vehicle started to pull away. "We'll have them good and tenderized by the time you guys go in after them." He waved as the HMMWV roared out the gate toward Riyadh.

Laliker turned and hurried back to his waiting scouts.

"Let's go catch our ride," he said, motioning toward Vestal's waiting TOW vehicles.

The scouts clambered up on the HMMWVs as Jeep slid in next to Vestal, who was eyeing him suspiciously.

"You trying to get word to Colley?" he asked, recognizing this to be the one conflict they hadn't yet discussed.

"Could be!" Jeep said, enjoying Vestal's discomfort and deciding he wouldn't relieve it. They might have buried the hatchet, but Laliker enjoyed knowing he still had a needle with which to prick his former adversary.

Vestal glared at him, then turned to Neuhaus. "Get us out of here, Private, before we start fighting again."

The TOW platoon joined up with the rest of D Company and made their way across the desert to an area near the Kuwait border. This was to be only one of many places they'd move to within the next few weeks, as all the ground forces began to shift back and forth around the border area in preparation for the attack.

McIver huddled in the rear sleeping, while Sommerhill sat listening to his Walkman. Since there was some news coming over AFN, he'd opted to tune into Milton Pope's program instead of playing a rap tape. Between records, the AFN DJ gave a running commentary, alternating between serious and humorous, on the air war. He listened as they rode along, wondering what life must be like for an Armed Forces disc jockey. He figured it must be pretty good, back there with all the celebrities on the rear veranda of the Dhahran International Hotel.

Just as his ambivalence was about to turn sour, Pope repeated a joke about Iraqi fighter pilots, and Sommerhill, laughing, formed a new conclusion. AFN disc jockeys might not be up to their asses in the sand like the other soldiers, he decided, but they were doing their job, boosting the morale of every swabbie, grunt and jet jockey in the theater of operations.

Eustas was proud of himself for coming up with that, and reached over to share his newfound maturity with Hallmark. The sergeant had followed McIver's lead, and was snoozing when Sommerhill shook his sleeve.

171

"What!?" he said, jolting from his nap. He looked over at Sommerhill and noticed the earphones. He snorted and gave the earpieces a yank, pulling them from Eustas's ears. "What do you want?"

Sommerhill retrieved the listening device, now dangling from Hallmark's hand and put it in his lap. "I've been thinking, Sarge," Sommerhill began.

"Oh no," Hallmark grumbled, "not again! OK, what about his time, Eustas?"

"About everybody doing their job!" he answered enthusiastically.

"Uh-huh."

"I mean, everyone has a job over here."

"That's right, Eustas. Cut to the chase," Hallmark said, impatiently.

"You're doing your job . . . I'm doing a job, right?"

Hallmark nodded, wary of where Sommerhill was taking him in the conversation. "Go on."

"McIver's!"

"What?" Hallmark stared down at the earpieces in Sommerhill's hand, thinking he might have pulled too hard and removed the corporal's brain.

"I'm doing a job formerly held by a sergeant. I should be getting a promotion, shouldn't I?" Sommerhill, dead serious, knotted his brows together as he stared into Hallmark's face.

"You know, Eustas," Hallmark said, reaching for a cigarette, "there's more to being a sergeant than

172

just being a hotshot gunner. You gotta show you've got professionalism and maturity."

"You aren't fixing to drag my ass over the coals for that Jodie call I pulled on El-T again, are you? Hey, Sarge, that was a long time ago."

"Less than a month ago," Hallmark corrected.

"Yeah? Well, a month over here is a long time. I've been doing some growing and I'd like some credit."

Flipping open his old Zippo, Hallmark lit his cigarette and exhaled a blue line of smoke across the HMMWV. "You're doing all right, Sommerhill. You've been watching your step fairly well, lately. It's got to be long-term, though. The question is, can you keep it up?"

Sommerhill moved uneasily on his seat. "Yeah, I can. I want a promotion, though."

Hallmark reached in his pocket and pulled out his notebook. Sommerhill, thinking he was going to write, handed him a pen. Surprised, Hallmark took the pen and put it in his pocket. "Thanks!"

"Wait," Sommerhill said, retrieving his pen. "I thought you wanted to write a reminder to promote me. I wasn't giving you my pen. What are you doing?" he asked, watching as the first sergeant thumbed through the pages.

"I wrote down some dates in here," Hallmark said, continuing to leaf. "Aha!" he said, stopping and pointing to a date next to Sommerhill's name. "Your four years are up next month, Eustas."

Quickly checking the date in his memory, Sommerhill nodded. "Yeah, so what?"

"Well, as I recall, in one of those moments last month, before you . . . 'grew' . . . you told me you'd be leaving this man's army as soon as this was over and we got back to the States."

Sommerhill flinched, but then grew defiant. "Well, I might change my mind, if I knew I was going to make sergeant."

Hallmark shrugged his shoulders. "No deals, Eustas. That ain't the way it works, and you know it!"

"OK." The corporal started to put the earpieces back in, figuring he and Hallmark had reached one of their famous impasses, then stopped. "But if you thought I deserved it, you'd promote me, right?"

"Sure!"

The answer seemed to satisfy him. He closed his eyes and continued to listen to the radio. McIver had been listening as the two men talked. As soon as he was sure Sommerhill couldn't hear him, he leaned forward and caught Hallmark's attention.

"He's been doing good, Van. It deserves some consideration," he said, backing Sommerhill's argument.

Hallmark nodded. "I'm thinking about it, Mac. Say, I thought you said he didn't like you?"

"Well, my stock seems to have risen. You were right, he's pretty damned smart."

"Yep," Hallmark said, "and he can be a real smart ass, too."

"He just don't always see things too clearly."

Hallmark laughed. "Well, your perception can be severely distorted when looking out of your navel. Maybe he's pulled his head out now."

CHAPTER TWENTY-FOUR

The smoke and sand grew thick inside the underground bunker where Tariq Shadi hunkered near the last of the remaining loot from the Fazid villa. This was the third day of continual bombardment by B-52 bombers. He knew, from the secondary explosions, that his intricate system of bunkers was taking heavy hits. An assessment of damage hadn't been possible due to sporadic flyovers by allied bombers and fighters.

Crouched in the dark recesses of his command bunker, he punched a number into his cellular phone and listened to the total silence on the receiver. There was no way he could reach headquarters in Baghdad. Nothing worked—not the radios, not the phones, nothing. Communications had been nonexistent between Shadi's brigade and Central Iraqi Command since the bombing started.

The bombing stopped after a few more minutes, and Shadi, choking on smoke and dust, worked his way to the front of the shelter. Bareem saw him moving in the haze and walked over to join him. The shelter was so small that both men had to walk bent over.

"Colonel Shadi," he called out. "It's me, Bareem. I'm over here."

The colonel squinted in the thick air and waited while Bareem shuffled sideways past a stack of rolled-up carpets. He coughed again, trying to clear his throat of the smoke.

"Are you all right?" Bareem asked as he stepped up beside him.

"Yes, but I need water. Let's get outside and see what the bombs have done before they come back," he said, pushing back on the heavy metal cover over the entrance to the bunker.

The sliding panel seemed to be stuck, so both men shoved again. The weight of mounds of sand, blown against the cover by the explosions, had the panel sealed. Fighting down panic, they shoved once more, and the metal door shook free. Finding a new opening, the sand cascaded into the shelter, threatening to seal them in again.

Bareem sank to his knees and began praying loudly. Shadi looked down at the officer with disgust. "Allah isn't going to save you! Get up before the men see you! They're digging us out now."

A hand poked through the sand as he spoke, and soon the passageway was clear. Two of the soldiers reached in and assisted Shadi out of the bunker. He turned and watched as they lifted Bareem, still visibly shaken, from the pit in the sand. He grabbed his second in command by the sleeve and pulled him close.

"Get control of yourself, Bareem!" he whispered harshly to the trembling man. "Get our people together. We have to move, and quickly!" He released Bareem and turned around to view the damage.

There were deep craters in the sand where his food and water supplies had been stored. A heavy column of smoke rose over one of his ammunition bunkers. The camouflage nets, spread over several of the destroyed tanks and BMPs, were still burning. Less that fifty of his men were out in the open; some appeared to be seriously wounded.

One line of bunkers, housing two of his infantry companies, had caved in. He could hear cries from the survivors as the rescuers dug through the sand. His engineers had little left to work with. Most of their massive earth-moving equipment had been destroyed. A small backhoe, stolen when they left Kuwait City, was in use now, freeing the trapped infantrymen.

"Water?" he asked one of the soldiers rushing past him toward the caved-in bunker. The man motioned to the right, behind the wreckage of the tanks. Shadi walked over and found the camouflaged truck under its sand-covered canopy. He grabbed a container next to the spigot and filled it. After quenching his thirst, he walked up the remaining wall of his earth berm and looked back over the defense he'd built.

More men worked their way out now, and he watched as they busily attended to the wounded. The defenses had been built in accordance to plans and specifications used in the Iran War, and as he looked over the ruins, Shadi knew it had been a mistake. The traditional defense posture, a series of triangles, the bases facing the enemy, with broad, deep antitank ditches, had made a clear target for the enemy bombers. Now the enemy had him plotted and marked, a new pinpoint on their target maps.

"Where," he mumbled out loud, "is our air defense?" Any good tanker knew air support was essential, and Tariq Shadi was a good armored officer, battle-tested and hardened by his many campaigns. As a veteran, though, he knew he didn't have time to worry about what had happened. More important now was to insure it wouldn't happen again.

He watched as the column of smoke from the burned tanks flowed westward over the sand. His eyes quickly looked beyond them, toward the horizon, where there were two Kuwaiti pumping stations. Excitedly he called out to an engineer officer near him.

"Shaheed! Quick, get up here."

The engineer turned and clamored up the side of the berm. "Sir?" he said as he reached Shadi.

"Take a platoon up there," Shadi pointed to the Kuwaiti oil plants, "and set fire to the stations. The smoke will provide cover from the bombers for our move and relocation."

The man saluted and rushed off the berm, calling out to several men as he left. Two BMPs lumbered up from their protected shelters, and the engineer, with his crew of demolition experts, loaded up and left for the pumping stations.

179

Shadi left the berm and continued with his plan for the new defenses. Two hours later he smiled as he heard the loud blasts from the oil refineries. He sprang back on the berm and watched the returning BMPs, even now dimly visible through the thick, oily smoke from the fires. The smoke, billowing and black, rolled over the sand, and soon the Iraqi Republican Guard Brigade was under its obscuring canopy.

As they moved to their new location, they could hear the sound of planes, even the whooping of attack helicopters, but could not tell if they were enemy or Iraqi. It no longer made a difference, as they were safe under the veil of the oily mantle overhead.

A ridge line appeared before them, and Shadi, standing in the lead jeep, signaled the speeding convoy toward its shelter. As soon as the tanks and equipment were under their camouflage, every able-bodied man became involved in the building of the defense.

The engineers restructured an antitank ditch to conform with the existing ridge line. The traditional four-meter-high berm plan of defense was replaced as two of their large earth-moving vehicles, now repaired, dug deep zigzag troop emplacements, again using the natural contours of the ridge. The armor revetments, previously centered in the old triangle defense, were moved into smaller circular formations scattered at random behind the zigzag infantry positions.

Occasionally the smoke would drift, leaving them exposed, but the men simply fell back into the shadows of the rock outcroppings and waited for the cover to return.

As they worked, Bareem found Shadi near the new ammunition bunker. The Iraqi colonel was obviously disturbed as he walked from one small pile to another. He looked up as Bareem approached.

"We need more ammunition," he said, swinging his arm around to show how little had been salvaged. "Send Khreem to Baghdad to requisition supplies."

"Yes," Bareem nodded, "and we need food and water also."

"We can't afford to have too large a convoy. Send someone else to Kuwait City for the water and food," Shadi said. "Tell them to take some of the commercial trucks of the Kuwaitis while they are there and come back in those. Less chance of being strafed by the enemy fighters."

"We need replacements for the men also, Colonel Shadi. Over half of our infantry was buried alive in that bunker."

Shadi gritted his teeth. "I would assume, when the ammunition and equipment is being replaced in Baghdad, we will also request more men. Think, Bareem!"

"Yes, sir," Bareem answered, nervously. "I was thinking of having the men pick up some Kuwaitis while in the city. We could use them to help."

"That's good," Shadi said, patting him on the shoulder. "Yes, do that. And gasoline, too. We need

181

to fill all the tanks and fighting vehicles. Yes, go now and arrange for resupply."

The Republican Guard from Shadi's command found very slim pickings in Kuwait City. Carefully targeted and marked positions had been blown up in the second day of bombing. The Kuwait partisans, aware that the Iraqis would be trying to resupply, had systematically burned and destroyed all food supplies. The water desalinization plant had gone up in smoke immediately after the bombing started.

The citizens of the city, aware that their liberation had begun, grew bolder. Iraqi soldiers fled for their lives down the narrow alleys, as Kuwaitis openly fired on them. The city, once unsafe for its own citizens, now became unsafe for the conquerors.

The Fazid brothers and the Special Forces team now occupied the back room of an old bakery. The team leader, still dressed in his Arab garb, shook hands with the older of the two brothers.

"Well," the American said, "I guess we'll be leaving now. We've got to go find some SCUD launchers and put stickers on them for our Air Force buddies." He released the man's hand and motioned his team out the door.

Before he left, he turned to the Fazids. "You take care now, you hear. I want to see you when we come back through for the victory celebration!"

The Kuwaiti partisan leader stepped over to him.

"You take care, too, my friend. Thank you, all of you, for your help."

"You are the heroes here," the American said, looking at the bedraggled but proud men. "You fought hard. Made this man's job a pleasure." He waved his hand and disappeared into the street.

Colonel Khalid, the regular army replacement for Commander Shadi in Kuwait City, looked out the window of a small store in the retail district of the city. He'd moved positions four times during the night. The city was now a hotbed of rebellion, stoked by the partisans' fires and the coalition's bombs. He'd had no chance to plan a strategy for reclaiming the city as he ran during the night, changing his command post from one hiding place to another. His scant military training had not prepared him for this.

Because of his sister's marriage to one of Saddam Hussein's brothers-in-law, he had been made a colonel. It was flattering to him at the time, certainly a step up in prestige from his professorship at Baghdad University. Now he desperately wished he were back in his safe classroom, far removed from this hell.

His command had scattered with the first bomb, taking with it all semblance of order. Somehow he had to get it back, to protect himself, if for nothing else.

Colonel Shadi had taken the bulk of the brigade with him when he left the city, and Gallenz, a well-trained Republican Guardsman, with the remnants of his regiment, now protected the airport and the docks. Khalid, like Shadi, wondered where the Iraqi Air Force was. Why they weren't shooting down the enemy? Why hadn't Gallenz at least sent up the Hinds, their Russian attack helicopters, to help him establish order in the city?

Communication was down, and he couldn't reach Baghdad, couldn't reach anyone. He looked across the room. Only two of his majors were there, along with three captains and a few soldiers. One of the soldiers, a sergeant he'd met during the night, was trying again to raise someone on their radio. He watched as the soldier grew more frustrated with each try.

"Anyone?" Khalid asked. "Have you reached anyone?"

"No, sir," the sergeant answered. "Everything's still dead."

Khalid grabbed one of the majors. "Go get some of the men. We need more protection. We will move into the hospital. The Americans won't bomb there. Hurry. We've got to get out of here," he said, listening to another wave of planes roaring overhead.

The major shook his head and darted out the door, seeking cover in each doorway as he worked his way down the street.

"Where does he think I'm going to get these men?" he said aloud, looking at the burning wreckage of the city. He knew most of them had run, tried to blend in with the Kuwaitis and other refugees moving around the city.

Khalid watched the major as he skittered down the street. This is impossible, he thought to himself. We all should leave, now. He ordered the move to the hospital.

Command Central was broken. While Colonel Khalid ran, Gallenz, decided to go on the offense. He couldn't get the Hinds up because of the enemy air strikes, but he could block an invasion on the sea. He called in some of his commandos.

"Go down to the loading pier. Dump the oil into the sea and set it on fire. That should stop any plan of the Americans to invade us over the water."

Satisfied with their coverage in that direction, he turned to his aide. "Assemble one company of infantry and a tank battalion. We're going to attack them at the border."

While Colonel Gallenz defended the airport and planned his attack on the Khafji area, eighty more Iraqi fighter bombers flew into Iran, seeking refuge from the air armada of the allied coalition. The Iranians allowed them to land, then confiscated the planes. The Iraqi Air Force was defeated.

Shadi was in a briefing with his tank commanders when Bareem interrupted.

"Sir, there's no food or water from Kuwait City. The convoy was attacked by partisans twice before they reached Colonel Gallenz at the airport. Colonel Khalid can't be found," Bareem said, unable to disguise the mounting fear in his voice.

Shadi stared at him in disbelief. "And the men, we did get some replacements, didn't we?"

"No, Gallenz refused to part with any. He kept the men we sent into town and allowed only a messenger to return. Gallenz wants you to join him. He's going to attack." Bareem watched Shadi's face turn red with rage.

"Attack?" Shadi said, shaking with anger. "His orders are to defend, not attack!" He turned from Bareem and fought for control. He walked out a few steps and turned. "Have we gotten anything from Baghdad yet?"

Bareem stared past Shadi, out to the horizon. "Nothing. We still can't reach them by phone or radio. No one has returned yet." Bareem dropped his voice to a whisper. "We don't have much water or food, sir. I've ordered it to be rationed out sparingly."

Shadi, hands behind his back, paced back and forth. "Yes. We don't need much food. We're not going to run out before we get supplies, but that's a good idea. Be careful with the water supply also. Have the men drain the fuel from all the civilian vehicles. Fill the tanks first, and hold the rest. Distribute all available ammunition." He stopped pacing and turned around. "Keep up the men's spirits. We are being tested and we will win!"

═══ CHAPTER TWENTY-FIVE ═══

D Company, 325th, had moved again. This time within spitting distance of the southeast corner of Kuwait. The sky overhead was heavily marked with jet trails, nothing new since the air war had started thirteen days ago. Rodwell called for an hour halt for lunch, and the men found shelter from the sun in the shadows of their stopped vehicles. Other than the jet trails, the sky was still clear, although the latest weather advisory warned of rains that night.

"Did you hear that?" McIver shouted to Vestal across the top of the HMMWV.

"What?" Vestal turned to face him, listening to some muffled blasts in the distance. "That must be the artillery doing a practice."

McIver shook his head. "No, sir. They aren't over there. It's too near Khafji and the air base. I wonder if they're taking SCUDs."

Overhead an Apache assault helicopter whooshed by, followed by three more, headed in the direction of the explosions.

"Whatever it is, they're about to have company," Hallmark said, joining Vestal. "Mac's right, that ain't artillery practice."

The Apaches continued over the horizon as D Company moved back into position across the desert. Laliker and his scouts, now the proud owners of four vehicles of their own, were to the east of the company as the choppers flew over.

Laliker didn't even notice the Apaches as he looked down at the map. "We're here," he said to Walker, seated next to him. "This is where we wait for the rest of the company."

"Wonder how long we'll be here," Walker said as the HMMWVs stopped.

Jeep grinned. "At least long enough to dig some pits for shelter." He opened the door and stepped out. "Let's get crankin'."

Walker sighed and slid out, joining him. "Another day of ditch diggin' in Saudi Arabia! This is the life, isn't it, sir?"

"At least we'll have a bath tonight, so we won't stink up our hooch." Jeep unfastened his entrenching tool and started to dig.

"You mean a Johnny Weissmuller shower?" one of the scouts said, walking past them.

"What's that?" Jeep turned to Walker.

Laughing, Walker replied, "That's what the men call the field showers. You know, the water's so cold it makes you yell like Tarzan."

Jeep nodded as he threw another spadeful of sand over his shoulder. "Keeps you from having any impure thoughts."

Walker stopped shoveling and stared at Laliker. "No it doesn't!"

"Hey," the scout who'd been digging next to them

said, dropping his spade and picking up his rifle. "What's that coming over that dune out there?"

Laliker and Walker both picked up their weapons and watched as four more figures joined the three already walking toward them.

"Marines!" one of the scouts shouted back to Laliker. "It's a Marine Recon bunch."

The men waved as they trudged across the dunes.

"Got any food?" one of the Marines shouted.

"Shell out the MREs," Walker said to the scout next to him. "Looks like we got company for lunch."

"Bummer! We thought you rear-echelon types would have some good grub," the first marine said, laughing as he walked up to Laliker. "Lance Corporal John Keyes, sir," he said, saluting, "United States Marines."

Laliker returned the salute. "How many men you got, Corporal?" he asked, watching as two more joined the seven already there.

"We're ten in all, sir. One of my guys likes to hang back a bit to make sure we ain't followed. He'll be here in a minute."

"Followed?" Laliker looked out over the sand. "Who'd follow you? Where the hell have you been?"

"We went over the border a ways. Our fly-boys said they hit an Iraqi brigade out there several days ago, but didn't see them after that. We went to check it out."

"Anything up there?"

"They was up there," Keyes said, accepting some water from Walker, "but they ain't now."

"You mean the bombers got an entire brigade?" one of the scouts said, followed by a loud "Hooah" from the others listening in.

"No, they done gone Elvis, like they just disappeared." Keyes held his hand up, cautioning the men around him. "We found a lot of damage up there, caved-in bunker that stunk to high heaven, full of bodies," he said, wrinkling his nose, "and a few burned-up tanks and BMPs, but there were also tracks going out of there. Lots of tracks."

"You didn't follow the tracks?"

"Nope," Keyes answered. "Wasn't in my instructions. Besides that, Lieutenant, there were *lots* of tracks, *tank* tracks. They sorta vanished into the smoke from the burning pump stations."

As he was talking, the last man from the Recon walked up to him. "Nothing on our tails," he reported to Keyes.

"Maybe they went back up to Baghdad," one of the scouts called out.

The Marine corporal shook his head. "Not these boys." He reached into a trouser pocket and pulled out a frayed, red triangular patch. "This," he said, holding the patch out for the scouts to see, "came off one of the bodies in the bunker. The boys up ahead of us are the *real* thing—the Iraqi Republican Guard. They just snuck off somewhere to regroup. We'll see them again."

The Marines helped as the scouts strung up some shelter halves between the two HMMWVs. The shade was a welcome relief as they sat down to eat, comparing different ways to make MREs more palatable. Within a short time they'd all agreed that a bottle of Tabasco on any of the Meals Ready to Eat made them edible, but never a pleasure. After they finished, Corporal Keyes walked out a few feet from the others and radioed back to Khafji for a pickup.

Walker watched as the man, smooth and steady up to now, suddenly leaned into the receiver and threw his hand to his head in surprise. Keyes replaced the receiver, but stood, stunned, as he stared out across the desert.

As the man turned back toward the others, Walker jumped up and hurried to him. "Something wrong?" he asked, grabbing Keyes by the shoulders.

Keyes stared at him, his face ashen. "It's started. My unit at Khafji was hit this morning by Iraqi tanks. We got casualties."

About that time, one of the scouts turned up his radio and AFN blared out the story of the Khafji raid. The battle was over, but so were the lives of eleven Marines. It was a long time before conversation started again, and when it did, it was the Marines, bitter and angry, complaining that they hadn't been there when their buddies were fighting.

"Yeah," Keyes said, at one point, "we *expected* trouble. We were across the border. Nobody thought anything would happen in Khafji yet."

Walker put his arm over Keyes's shoulder. "It was like that in Panama," he said to the shaken young Marine. "The places you felt the safest were usually the most dangerous."

An hour later a Huey dropped in to pick up the Recon group and carry them back. Anxious for news of the battle, Laliker talked with the pilot while the Marines loaded.

He, too, looked ashen as he rejoined the scouts, the Huey stirring up sand in its flight behind him.

"Friendly fire," he said, looking at Walker. "The Huey pilot said word is that of the eleven casualties, seven were hit by friendly fire."

"Shit!" Walker spit in the sand. "The fighting must have been close. They hit by artillery?"

"I don't know. Chopper pilot said it could have been from an Apache. Said it was a surprise, that the Egyptians up on the border reported Iraqi tanks trying to surrender. The Iraqis had their turrets turned around backward, showing nonaggression. Egyptians let them pass through, but when the tanks got closer, they swung the turrets and started firing. The Marines scrambled, called in air and launched a helluva defense. The fight got 'up close and personal.'"

"Damn!" Walker shook his head, "They didn't have anything to blow off those tanks except air and artillery. When it gets that close, you're probably shit out of luck anyway. God bless those guys. That's gonna be hard for their folks back home to understand."

An hour later D Company pulled over the horizon and started preparing camp with the scouts. The Marines, usually the butt of good-natured jokes, were remembered that night in quiet reverence as the chaplin held a prayer service on the dunes.

Laliker found Vestal and told him what the Recon group had seen up north.

"No shit," Vestal said, rubbing his chin. "Republican Guard. Did they say how big they thought the unit might be?"

Laliker shook his head. "Nope, just that there were many tank trails leading out of there."

Vestal looked toward the border. "I wonder if they're still up there. Maybe our bombers have found them by now."

"Headquarters wants us, me and my scouts, to give it a quick look tomorrow and send them a report. Looks like I'm going to beat you over the border," Laliker said, wiping sand from his eyes.

"Yeah, I already heard that. We're supposed to meet up with the French 6th Armored Division sometime tomorrow," Vestal said, laughing. "Gonna do a practice to insure our units mesh."

"That's good, though," Laliker said. "It'll give you a chance to talk to those Frenchies and get some pointers on how to improve your technique with women!"

"I haven't had any complaints."

"That's not what I've heard."

Vestal smiled and shrugged. "Did they say how long you'll be up north?"

"Yep. At least they said for us to stop digging in here. Rodwell said to make a radio check every day at ten hundred hours on differing frequencies. He'll tell us where to go from there."

"Did he tell you before or after you dug your hooch?"

"Before. Why?"

"I was thinking of offering to lease it from you. You and Walker make a damn nice place," Vestal said, smiling. "Looks like you guys have perfected ditch digging."

"Actually," Laliker said, going along with him, "I taught Walker everything he knows. I took Ditch Digging 101 at A&M. What's the matter? You mean they didn't offer it at the Point?"

"They did," Vestal replied, walking back to his HMMWV to pick up his ruck, "but I opted for something that left my fingernails clean."

"I knew it wasn't auto repair!" Laliker yelled as Vestal walked away.

═══ CHAPTER TWENTY-SIX ═══

Sweeping the sand ahead of them with portable mine sweepers, the scout platoon moved carefully across the border, heading for their objective. When they reached the tank ditch, they found that the Air Force's bombs had caused many of the mines to detonate. Alert and wary, they followed behind the mine sweepers.

The Republican Guard position was exactly as the Marine Recon unit had described it. The bodies in the bunker had ripened a bit more, and the place buzzed with fat, black flies. Walker radioed back their findings while Laliker and the others looked around.

"How many do you figure were in there, Lieutenant?" one of the scouts asked, walking away from the cave-in.

Laliker shook his head. "Hard to say, but I'd guess it was at least a company, maybe more."

As they walked around the abandoned Iraqi position, Jeep was struck by how big it was. The traditional Iraqi fighting position was a triangle, with a company of infantry in each point, armor in the center. This wasn't just one triangle; it had been at least three, with deep tank trenches stretching the length of their two-thousand-meter bases.

"Hey, Lieutenant!" one of the men taking an inventory of the abandoned vehicles called out. "Come look at this."

Jeep walked over to join him next to a T72M1. The big Russian-made tank was now a black, burned wreck. Even in its burned-out state, it was impressive. This was the first one Jeep and his scouts had seen, other than in training manual pictures.

Laliker glanced down to where the scout pointed out a bumper marking.

"I thought the Guard had red patches," the man said, looking down at the triangle with green marking.

Jeep turned and yelled at Walker, who was still on the radio. "Tell them the position has a T72M1 wreck with the markings of the 2nd Republican Guard!" He turned back to the man next to him. "Good work. Now we know who they were."

Laliker continued to look over the tank. He climbed under the front end and inspected the front panels, then carefully hoisted himself over the side and into the turret. After a few minutes he emerged. Walker had finished the commo session and was standing next to the tank as Laliker climbed back down.

"You remember the TOW guys talking about the '72," he said, scratching a fleabite.

"Yeah, vaguely," Walker answered.

"They had to carry two types of missiles, because

the Charlie series they were using was supposedly detectable by the T72M1s."

"Yeah, the Delta is supposed to be so new they wouldn't have had time to make the adaptation. So what?" Walker asked, puzzled.

"Well, I'm not a tank systems expert, but I'm damned if I can see any detection devices in there. At least this one doesn't have any. When you radio in again, have them pass the information on to the TOW crews." Laliker found another flea. "Damn, who would have thought the fleas would survive the explosion," he said, scratching furiously. "The control pit in there must be jumpin' with them!"

"Prepare for meltdown," Walker said, pulling an olive drab can of insect repellent from his pack and spraying Jeep.

"Don't hit my sunglasses; that shit eats plastic!"

Walker returned the spray to his pack and looked out over the destroyed bunkers. "This place give me the willies. How many of their vehicles did we count?"

Jeep looked down at the list the scout had handed him. "Fifteen tanks, eight BMPs, two Scorpions, a BTR-50 and assorted engineer equipment. Of the fifteen tanks, only one T72M1, three more of the old 72s; the rest were T54s and T6911s."

Walker whistled. "Bit outfit! What do you figure, a full brigade?"

"No, not quite, but more than a battalion. At least before the bombing."

Both men looked out over the smoky horizon as they talked. All the Kuwaiti wells had been torched now, and thick oily smoke filled the air. Both knew that the 2nd Regiment of the Guard had taken a hard hit, had retreated to fight again and was out there somewhere.

As they stood there, rain began to fall, first in light sprinkles, then in a torrent, driven by the strong winds. Laliker signaled everyone back into the HMMWVs, and they started out, the mine sweepers plodding along in front of the vehicles. At a spot two kilometers east of the abandoned site, they waited in the HMMWVs for a break in the storm, then unloaded and made camp.

Rain fell steadily for the next ten days. The scouts continued to work over the border, reporting in daily. As dawn broke on the morning of the eleventh day, the radio crackled. Division was calling to set up a rendezvous. The 82nd was on a move-out, this time in battalion strength.

This was the news the scouts had been waiting for. Morale and enthusiasm were high as they sped back to the rendezvous point.

CHAPTER TWENTY-SEVEN

Helicopters swarmed like flies over the 325th as they loaded the men and equipment. The sand didn't tamp down much, even with the falling rain, and swirled heavily around the large assemblage.

Laliker, his face wrapped in a scarf and wearing goggles to protect his eyes from the wind, walked up to Vestal as the TOW platoon leader watched his equipment being hoisted. "We're out next," he said, tapping him on the shoulder. "See you in Iraq!"

Vestal turned and nodded, giving him a pat on the back as the scout walked away and joined the others being loaded onto the CH-47.

"I just hope they don't screw up my shit so bad I can't fix it."

Vestal looked over at Sommerhill, standing beside him. "Don't worry. When they drop those HMMWVs, the tires won't even jiggle."

McIver, standing behind them, snorted with disbelief. "Sure!" he sputtered. "And we ain't going to Iraq! Don't you believe that, Sommerhill. We'll be zeroing the sights the minute that thing quits bouncing."

"Lieutenant Vestal!"

Vestal spun around, coming face-to-face with Captain Rodwell. "Yes, sir."

"You get your boys on the second chopper. I'll be in the third. Let's get crackin'."

Hallmark watched as the men got into the big twin-rotor CH-47. They were ready now, as ready as they would ever be. They all seemed eager, even Sommerhill. Hallmark boarded behind Vestal and sat down next to him. After they lifted off, he turned to the lieutenant.

"Well, this is it. We're finally going to get to do some of that 'kicking ass and taking names' Colonel Nixon talked about back at Pope last August," he said, lighting a cigarette.

"August," Vestal said, looking back at him, "and now it's February. It's been a long wait. I'm glad it's over."

"Yeah, it has been." Hallmark exhaled. "You see those Rangers that came in last night?"

"Affirmative. I know a couple of them. Laliker and I met them in training school down in Florida."

"Three companies of the 2nd Ranger Battalion are going in with us," Hallmark said, as they watched an Apache swoop past and ahead of them. "I like the smell of this, Lieutenant. It's definitely going to be fun, 'cause we've invited all the right people to the party."

Unloaded and on the ground, each of the company commanders assembled their men for a briefing. Rodwell stood the men at ease as he fought the wind whipping at his map easel. "This is our location. The 504th is here, at An Nasariyah. The

505th is over in the Rumalia oil fields," he said, tapping the map with his pointer. "The road over there" he said, pointing to the highway nearby, "junctions at this point. Intelligence says there's a headquarters there, near this small town." He pointed to Ur, several kilometers to the southwest, and continued. "Probably the new headquarters of the remaining Republican Guards. The Rangers will go forward and assault that position with us close behind to deliver the knockout punch."

He took a deep breath. "Check out your vehicles, weapons and commo systems immediately and be prepared to move out in an hour. If we know the enemy's position, he might know ours. We're on the offense now, and let's keep it that way. You're dismissed, except for the TOW platoon leaders."

Vestal and the others remained as the rest of the Company followed their NCOs back to get their gear ready.

"OK," Rodwell said, "listen up, here. How many of your vehicles are working, Vestal?" he asked as the men huddled around him.

"Five, sir. My first sergeant says the other one will crank by the time we have to go, though."

"Good. I hope so. Here's where I want you to place the Virgins." He pointed to a spot near the single major highway running south from Basra to Kuwait. "Get them in position as soon as possible. You will stop any armor units that might decide to come down to help out their buddies in Kuwait."

"Yes, sir," Vestal said, looking at the map. "Will we have artillery support?"

201

Rodwell licked his lips. "Arty is going to be alerted for the Ranger assault, but the answer is yes, if you need it."

Vestal nodded. "I take it you're not expecting heavy traffic on the road."

"Not really, but be prepared for anything. Good luck, Lieutenant," Rodwell said, dismissing him. "I'll see you in Baghdad."

As Vestal zigzagged between men and equipment toward his platoon, he heard the loud pop of an engine firing. He smiled as he heard it begin to rev steadily. His sixth HMMWV was working again as he joined his platoon.

"OK!" he exclaimed. "Let's go kick some butt. Hallmark, you're riding with me."

They slid into their waiting vehicle and led their company toward the road. As they rode along, Vestal pointed out to Hallmark their new position on the map, and he busily marked it on his own.

"I got it, El-T," Hallmark said, carefully folding his map and putting it away. "Looks like a good place to be."

Vestal tilted his head toward Sommerhill. "What's with him?" he asked, watching as the corporal worked on the sights to the system. "He got a problem?"

"Not really," Hallmark answered, lighting a cigarette. "He just likes to get his shit straight."

"Shit straight?" Vestal gave him a puzzled look.

"Yeah, he's real serious about this. It was a good move to make him a gunner." Hallmark eased back, enjoying his smoke.

"Speaking of 'good move,' you got this HMMWV purring like a kitten. You didn't tell me you were a mechanic."

Hallmark exhaled deeply. He knew where this conversation was going. "I'm a damned good mechanic, El-T, but if you're looking for help on that old truck of yours, you can forget it."

Vestal looked hurt. "I thought we were friends."

"We are friends, but that truck of yours is straight out of *The Grapes of Wrath*. It's a welfare truck."

"Yeah?" Vestal looked at him. "And what's that mean?"

"It works if it wants to," Hallmark said, stubbing out his cigarette.

The Apache that hovered overhead, escorting the TOW platoon to their location, turned and veered back southward as the first of the HMMWVs pulled into position.

The terrain was covered with high dunes and peculiar rock formations that jutted up from the sand. Prickly shrubs and cacti grew over some of the dunes and clung stubbornly to rock faces.

The highway, nothing more than a two-way road at this point, wound through the established dunes and outcrops like a snake.

The rain had ceased right after they left the staging area, but the clouds remained overhead. Now, as the unit dug in two kilometers apart from the road, the sun, having never made an appearance all day, set.

Vestal was in the northernmost HMMWV and

the last to pull into position behind a dune. On the far horizon they could see UH-60 Blackhawks ferrying howitzers to the artillery unit behind them. As the light died, the winds shrieked around them, drying the sand and chilling the soldiers to the bone.

"Should we give them to him now?" McIver asked Hallmark, pointing to the objects underneath some poncho liners in the back of the HMMWV.

"Give him what?" Vestal asked.

"Oh, just a little something Laliker lifted from the Marine Recondos. He sent them over to you as a gift," Hallmark said.

Vestal watched as McIver pulled away the liner, revealing two Marine Corps MK-19 grenade launchers.

Hallmark grinned as a stunned Vestal looked them over.

"He said we might need them. They are right handy. We can get them mounted if you wish."

"I *wish*! Pull them out here and let's get started."

They pulled the vehicle-mount automatic grenade launchers out of the HMMWV and unwrapped them as the others sat inside watching.

Sommerhill cleared his throat. "Since they aren't really ours, I'd like to request them after the war. We've had some trouble in our neighborhood back home and I—"

"Get out of here, Eustas!" McIver interrupted, laughing. "You know, you're becoming a real psychopath since I taught you how to kill tanks."

"I know." Sommerhill beamed. "Isn't it great!"

"Holy shit! We got company!"

Everyone turned as Neuhaus pointed down the road. In the last rays of twilight, they could see two Iraqi BTR-50s, escorted by a French-made Panhard AML armored car, rounding the dune up ahead.

The Iraqis had spotted them, and the AML sped forward, its turret-mounted gun seeking a target. Vestal and Hallmark, armed only with their M-16s, dove for cover, yelling for Neuhaus to get into action.

A 90-mm shell hurtled toward them, as the Iraqis fired. The round hit and detonated well to the left of Vestal's HMMWV as Neuhaus turned to give Eustas a clear shot.

Sommerhill's hands were shaking as he adjusted the sights. He took a deep breath, lined up the AML in his cross hairs and fired. The TOW screamed out over the sand and hit, flipping the Panhard skyward as it exploded.

One of the BTRs pulled to cover behind a large rock formation as the other, still on the road, screeched to a halt. The hatch opened, and twenty infantrymen jumped out, firing as they hit the ground.

Vestal's second TOW vehicle fired and hit the exposed BTR. The explosion took out five men, but the Iraqis were now closer to them, firing AK-47s and 9-mm Sterling submachine guns. Two of the soldiers stopped, placed the SGM medium machine gun they carried into the sand and opened the ammo canister.

Vestal and Hallmark scurried behind a patch of shrubs and pulled their rifles forward, watching as the TOWs worked their magic.

Bullets were now zinging over their heads and ricocheting off the skin of the HMMWV. The Iraqis with the machine gun pulled the ammo belt out of the canister and loaded.

Sommerhill fired another TOW toward the hiding BTR, unable to see if it did any damage as the air filled with sand. The stone outcrop had protected it; the TOW glanced off the rock and detonated in the air.

"It's a miss!" Neuhaus howled.

"Shit!" Sommerhill said, watching as the BTR jerked from cover, its tracks pulling up chunks of road as it turned back north.

"Holy hell," Neuhaus yelled, "he's going for help. Hit him! Stop him!"

"Now I got you, sucka." Sommerhill fired. The BTR didn't have a chance. The missile struck. The tracked personnel carrier flipped up on one end and turned upside down as it exploded.

The Iraqis had their machine gun going now, firing as Neuhaus swerved up on the road and pulled the HMMWV back behind a dune. Sommerhill had dropped down into the belly of the vehicle and grabbed an M-16 and some grenades. Neuhaus jumped out and was firing, giving him cover.

"The Sarge and El-T are pinned down by that machine gun. We gotta get it!" Sommerhill said, crawling up the dune for a better view.

"Watch out!" Neuhaus loosed a burst from the

M-16 as an Iraqi stood up behind Sommerhill. The man fell forward and slid back down the side of the dune.

McIver dropped for cover behind some cactus. He yelled up at Sommerhill, "Hold where you are, Eustas! I've got 'em! Cover me!" He stood amid the flying bullets and hoisted the AT-4 launcher up on his shoulder. He fired, sending the two Iraqis and their machine gun into their Muslim seventh heaven.

Hallmark and Vestal fired steady bursts at the two remaining Iraqis advancing toward them over the dune.

As their targets fell, all firing stopped. Silence moved over them like a vacuum.

McIver, rolling side over side across the road, settled next to Hallmark. "What's happening out there?" he said, pointing toward the now flaming vehicles.

Hallmark shook his head and continued to stare out across the illuminated scene before him. After a few minutes more of quiet, he crawled out to Vestal. "I think that's it, El-T," he said, rolling over on his back.

Vestal was breathing heavily, feeling the rush of adrenaline. He turned his head and watched as Hallmark lit a cigarette.

"That's it?"

"Yep, I think we got 'em. Let's give it a while, but I heard Neuhaus on the radio. We'll have air in here in a minute. I figure anything left after our pounding, the Apaches can police up."

"How can you smoke? Man, I can hardly breath," Vestal said, wiping sweat from his forehead. "By the way, McIver, pretty fancy shooting with the AT-4."

"Give me anything with a trigger and I'm a happy man."

Sommerhill remained atop the dune a few minutes more, then rolled down, past the dead Iraqi, to the HMMWV.

Lying on the ground, Neuhaus finished his radio transmission and turned over to Sommerhill in the goat grass next to him. His face was still flushed with excitement.

"It got a little close out there," he said, panting.

"Yeah, it did," Sommerhill answered. "Thanks for watching my back."

"Forget it," Neuhaus said. Then he raised himself up on one elbow. "Eustas, what was the first thing you thought of when it started?"

"I thought, I gotta pee," he smiled, "and I still do."

Hallmark was right. It was over. The bright lights from the hovering aircraft displayed the bodies of the Iraqi infantrymen and their wrecked vehicles. Vestal's platoon needed a new name. They weren't virgins anymore.

Sommerhill strutted around the HMMWV. "I'm bad, I'm bad!"

"That's right, son. Now, let's get this mounted," Hallmark said, pointing to the M-19, "and it'll make you the baddest man south of Baghdad. We'll put the other one on later."

"Hurry," Vestal said. "We need to move our position now and get set up again."

Working quickly, they put the automatic grenade launcher in place. Hallmark and Sommerhill threw their tools back into the vehicle and jumped in.

Vestal slid in next to McIver as the HMMWVs roared off to set up again at a point twenty kilometers away on the road.

The second M-19 was mounted on the vehicle behind them. After the TOW platoon dug in at its new location, they took turns dozing in the HMM-WVs. The wind outside had picked up, and they battened down for the threatening sandstorm. Neuhaus complained several times about the breakup in transmissions on the radio.

CHAPTER TWENTY-EIGHT

The Rangers launched their attack on the Republican Guard headquarters at 0300 hours. The Iraqis, sleeping fitfully in the predawn hours, were caught unawares. Their perimeter guards, shaken by the bombings of the previous day, were hunkered down in their makeshift shelters dozing. The Rangers found them and made sure their slumber was deep and permanent.

Two platoons of Rangers low-crawled across the sand to one of the main Iraqi billets and surrounded the building. When their troops were in place, the platoon leaders gave the signal to start the attack.

Seven LAWs, fired directly into the building, gave the sleeping Iraqis their early morning wake-up call.

Pandemonium followed as the surviving Guardsmen rushed out the exits, to be greeted by a hail of bullets from the Rangers' automatic weapons.

The mortars came in next, pounding away at the area around the command bunkers, toppling their already faulty communications satellite dish.

As Iraqis in the headquarters bunker and other billets, shaken from their beds by the mortars and grenades, realized they were under fire, they sprang for their weapons. Confused and disoriented, their leaders shouted out conflicting instructions to the frightened soldiers, further delaying the defense.

The commander of the billets next to the motor pool was first to gain control, sending his men out to their fighting vehicles. Two Scorpions sputtered to life, then spun out to meet the attacking Rangers, only to be blown apart at the gate by Ranger AT-4s.

The explosions caused a number of secondary blasts as several surrounding the small Alvis Saracen tanks, their gas tanks and ammo racks full, ignited. The Saracens erupted, scattering pieces of molten steel and burning men into the surroundings. The exit from the motor pool was blocked by burning wreckage.

One of the Rangers carrying a AT-4 nudged his buddy. "This is like shooting little fish in a barrel."

As he spoke, a Cascavel, unable to move forward, swiveled its 90-mm gun turret around sharply. The Ranger sighted him, locked in the target and thumbed the trigger, sending the missile spiraling out. It connected, blasting the fighting vehicle before it had time to fire.

With the motor pool ablaze, the entire area was lit up even more. The Rangers then set off charges on the arsenal. The resounding blasts sent tons of sand and metal high into the sky. Falling debris landed everywhere, setting the perimeter walls and outbuildings on fire.

Iraqis ran from the incinerated buildings, some

firing wildly into the night. The Rangers waited and picked them off quickly as the enemy blundered into their kill zones.

To the right of the arsenal was a series of buildings, its roofs painted with bright red crescents, the symbol of the Arab Red Cross. The buildings were assumed to be a hospital complex. Suddenly the walls fell forward as six tanks, hidden inside, roared through toward the Rangers.

Although they had seen no tanks and none had been reported from aerial observation, the Rangers were anticipating surprises. The radioman calmly gave the position to one of the 82nd's artillerymen on the line, then ducked for cover, yelling out loudly, "Fire in the hole!"

The Rangers tucked and rolled as the first barrage came in, causing the ground to shake, but falling short behind the tanks. Untouched, the armored vehicles continued to lumber forward through the motor pool, climbing up over the wrecked vehicles.

A T72 led the five older T62s in the assault. The three-man crew inside the lead vehicle was already firing its 7.62-mm gun at the Rangers, the massive main turret swinging around, preparing to deliver its 125-mm shell.

The commo man reported the short hit, rapidly telling the artilleryman on the line to "adjust and fire for effect," then dropped back to the ground and waited for the "King of Battle" to loose his thunderbolts.

The next artillery rounds, already in the tubes, thundered out, causing a seismic sensation as they found their mark, time and time again, pounding the tanks to luminescent rubble.

All activity in the Iraqi area ceased. There were occasional pops as the arsenal continued to send flames licking high into the dark morning sky, but the battle was over.

The Rangers waited and watched as the overwhelmed fortress of the Republican Guard fell in on top of itself.

"Look," a Ranger captain said, as another building emptied. "They're surrendering! Don't fire on them; they've got a white flag."

The Iraqi soldiers, obviously terrified, stumbled blindly toward the Rangers, choking from the smoke. They came forward with their hands high over their heads, some still holding weapons. The one waving the white flag was crying and talking at the same time.

"Shit," the Ranger captain grumbled as he watched them coming. "This isn't going to work. Call Jones up here. He speaks Arabic, doesn't he?"

Hearing his name, Jones ran up to the captain.

"Talk to these guys, Jones," the captain urged.

"*Qiff! Ilqi Slaahak!*" he yelled in Arabic, telling the Iraqis to halt and lay down their weapons.

The soldiers stopped and dropped their guns at their feet. Several of the Rangers, well covered by the others, hurriedly picked them up and threw them over to the side.

"Great!" The captain was impressed. "Now tell them they're our prisoners, hands up and sit down."

213

Jones nodded. *"Inta Sajeen, irfaa idak ijlis!"* he said.

As the Iraqis sat with their hands over their heads, one of them yelled out, *"Akil! Akil!"*

The captain stepped over to Jones. "What's he saying?"

Jones reached into his BDU pocket and threw the man a package of MRE dried peaches.

"They want food." Both men watched as several of the prisoners tried to catch the package. The Iraqi who finally ended up with it tore it open with his teeth, scattering the dried fruit over the ground. Immediately a struggle ensued as the men around him fought one another for the pieces.

"Jeez, they're starving. Go get some MREs, open the packs and distribute them as far as they'll go. Jones, you stay with them and find out as much as you can. See if they have any wounded." The Ranger captain turned and called for the commo sergeant.

"Sir?" A tall, skinny Ranger with a commo pack walked up, eyeing the Iraqis on the ground with suspicion.

"Get on the horn and ask what we're supposed to do with these guys. Damn it, the last thing I needed was a bunch of hungry prisoners."

Squatting down next to the prisoners, the translator talked with them. After a few minutes, the Iraqis relaxed, and all of them tried to talk to him at once. Calming them down, Jones pointed from one to another, and each man shook his head "Yes."

"What are they saying?" the Ranger leader asked Jones.

Jones stood, signaling the Iraqis to remain seated, and walked back over to his commander. "This bunch, or most of them anyway, aren't Republican Guard. They're conscripts from Baghdad—students, bellhops, bus drivers, cooks. They'd never been soldiers until a month ago. They were taken down here and told to fight or die. The Republican Guard made them stay with death threats against their families."

"Damn," the captain said, staring at the pathetic men as they quickly accepted the food being distributed. "They act hungry."

"Oh," Jones said, "they aren't acting. Seems they haven't had much food since late December. Food is being rationed in Baghdad, and they've received no resupply since the bombing started down here. They're happy as clams that we're here."

The skinny commo sergeant returned and stood next to Jones, listening as the translator spoke, but keeping his rifle trained on the prisoners.

"Well?" the Ranger captain asked.

"Seems there's a bad sandstorm headed our way. They'll send vehicles or choppers out to pick us up as soon as the weather permits. We're to start back, using the highway, with our prisoners."

Shaking his head, the captain looked down at his watch. "Well, it'll be dawn in an hour. We're going to make slow progress with these guys and a storm. Let's get moving."

The headquarters was completely neutralized.

The Rangers had four men with minor injuries, no dead, and thirty-five prisoners. They started their long march back to the 325th, making the Iraqis lead the way across the sand, hands on heads.

As they walked along, the winds shifted from the south, blowing so hard the men leaned into them for balance. The sand, now dry, began to stir. The Rangers signaled a halt and hurriedly dug in for the storm.

Soon all visibility ceased. Everything turned tan as the wind whipped the sand into a thickened frenzy.

The Rangers, after several tries on the radio, reached the 325th to report their position and were told to stay where they were. The storm was worse than had been predicted.

CHAPTER TWENTY-NINE

Jeep Laliker's scout platoon was being held in reserve back at the battalion staging area. All day he had hung around the commo tent, listening to communiqués as they came in. Things were happening out there, and he wanted to be part of it.

His impatience was beginning to get the better of him as he fought his way through the wind to Captain Rodwell's tent. Rodwell was just leaving as Laliker called out to him.

"Sir! I need a word with you."

Rodwell, leaning into the wind, motioned Jeep into the tent. He grabbed the flap and tied it down, then turned to him.

"What's your problem, Laliker?" he asked, dusting himself off.

"I want a job, sir. My men and I are being left out."

Rodwell sat down on the edge of his cot and loosened his boot laces. "Look, I've got my own problems. We've lost commo in several places. Your buddy Vestal and his boys had a little action today, and we've only reached them once since they moved. Hell, Battalion can't get out to pick up the Rangers, and they've got prisoners . . . and now you're telling me you feel left out! Kwityerbitchin', as my old mama would say."

"OK, sir, but hear me out. The sandstorm has all aircraft down for a while, right?" He watched Rodwell nod in agreement, then continued. "And it's fouling up communication. The commo boys are worried that it might be screwed up for a while, even after the storm, because of the sand."

Rodwell waved his hand impatiently. "If you have a point, make it!"

Laliker stepped closer. "If the aircraft and the commo are your eyes and ears, you've lost them. There's no way to gather intelligence. That's a mission for scouts. We can make it through this storm and be out forward tomorrow when this thing breaks."

"You really want out there, don't you? What makes you think I'd consider sending you, in this storm?"

"Because we're the last, best chance you've got, sir," Jeep said, squaring his jaw. "Our vehicles are outfitted with unique equipment, giving us maximum efficiency in this situation."

Rodwell stopped unlacing his boots and stared down at the sand. He knew Laliker's new HMM-WVs were outfitted with Global Positioning Systems and LORANs, which would give an accurate location even in the hostile weather. "How will you get word back, if you see anything?"

"I'll continue to try the radios. Failing that, I'll send a man back in the HMMWV. It'll work, sir. Let us go."

Rodwell threw his hands up. "OK, I'll do it. But I want you to try to find Vestal. There's a hell of a fight planned for tomorrow down in Kuwait. The 1st Armored is going after the Republican Guard, and the Iraqis might just try to run to Baghdad. If they do, they'll run straight into Lieutenant Vestal."

"Yes, sir." Laliker started to leave.

"Wait a minute. Your communications are mounted in the HMMWV, right?"

"That's affirmative, sir."

"Get a couple of pack jobs, in case you have to leave the vehicles. I want you to get out there and see what's happening. Draw supplies and ammo for a week. Get extra gas, then get back in here and I'll show you where to go."

"Yes, sir!" Laliker snapped a salute and turned into the tent flap, almost shaking the tent loose. Embarrassed, he fumbled with the tied closure. "Sorry about that," he mumbled as Rodwell stared at his departing back.

The scouts were ready to go. Laliker and Walker met with Rodwell to get the coordinates on Vestal's platoon.

"He should be here." Rodwell bent over the map. "This is where they were moving to, after their brush with the Iraqis. We got broken messages from them after that, but enough to know they're OK."

"Yes, sir," Laliker said, imprinting the location on his mind. "We'll find them and scout the area."

219

"Don't be a hero out there. Those new HMMWVs are hot shit, but they aren't tank killers!"

"No, sir, I'll let the Virgins handle that little detail."

"The storm seems to be blowing in and out. You've got a little clearing now." Rodwell stepped quickly over to the tent flap, untied it and held it open for Jeep and Walker. "Please, Laliker, allow me. Good luck!"

Laliker and Walker jumped into the lead vehicle and took off, through the sand and wind, toward Vestal's company.

With wind gusting so hard at times it seemed to lift them off the road, and visibility limited, progress was slow. The road had disappeared under the blowing sand. Laliker worked from a compass and map, writing down the information each time he checked, to provide a record. He thumbed in the GPS to prove his data.

Walker, riding next to him, watched as Laliker studiously navigated through the sandstorm. Not bad work for a kid, he thought, admiring the lieutenant's skills.

"They teach you that in Ranger school?"

"Nope, my dad used to make us do this every time we went camping or backpacking. I guess I learned how to use a compass when I was ten or eleven." Jeep flipped off his Mag-lite and leaned back. "We're where we think we are."

The HMMWV progressed at a slow speed, never able to exceed 10mph. Blowing trash would occasionally soar by.

Walker laughed as an empty MRE carton bounced off the hood of the HMMWV. "Look," he said as the box blew out of sight again. "With the wind blowing from the south, that thing will be in Baghdad before we are. Just a little reminder to Hussein that the Americans are here."

"Damn." Neuhaus slammed the door to the HMMWV and looked over at Vestal. "We got major problems with the antennas. Seems like they suffered some damage in the fight back there, but the sand and wind are making it hard to repair. That's why we're having problems reaching battalion."

"Can it be repaired?" Vestal asked.

"Sure," McIver said from the back, "if this wind stops and we have some time to work on it."

"OK, then, first priority when we get a break is to get commo up and running." Vestal looked over at McIver. "I'll try to get back to our other vehicles and see how they're coming."

Hallmark tumbled out of the seat, into the wind. "You lead, sir. I'll go with you."

Sommerhill sat in the back of the HMMWV rereading a letter he'd pulled from his pocket. He'd been strangely subdued since his initial outburst after the fight. As Hallmark and Vestal left to go check on the out TOWs, he folded the letter and stuffed it back into his pocket.

He stepped over the seats and past McIver, who was busily working on a piece of the antenna, and sat down next to Neuhaus.

"Hi, Eustas, what's going on?" Neuhaus asked, facing him as he leaned back against the door.

"I was thinking," Sommerhill began slowly. "You know, about what happened back there."

"Yeah?" Neuhaus looked at him.

"I just wanted to thank you again for covering me. I didn't even see that guy."

"No problem," Neuhaus said. "You get some mail before we left?" He had noticed him earlier with the letter.

Sommerhill nodded and turned his face away. "From Kisha."

"Want to talk about it?"

McIver continued to work on the antenna but leaned forward to listen to the conversation in front of him. Eustas was his star gunner, and he knew the man was upset when they left battalion. If Sommerhill had a problem, it could affect them all.

"The bitch has divorced me. Is a Mexican divorce legal in America?" he blurted out.

"Jeez!" Neuhaus sat up straight. "Mexican divorce? I thought she was in North Carolina."

"Not anymore. Seems she left for California around Thanksgiving with the Reverend Doctor Willie Abdul Kinzobar Johnson, the 'Divine Disciple' of the damned crazy church group she joined."

McIver set the antenna to one side and looked up at him. The man's shoulders slumped forward in a posture of despair, his head in his hands. Silence followed Sommerhill's news as Mac and Neuhaus struggled for something to say.

Finally Sommerhill broke the silence. "What do I do?" he said, raising his head.

"Hey, Eustas." Neuhaus reached over to pat the man's shoulder. "I'm sorry."

"What about that Mexican divorce, will it stand up . . . in court, I mean? You're the lawyer."

"Whoa!" Neuhaus stopped him. "*Pre-Law* is as far as I got, and not very far at that, but I do know, from clerking at the firm, that the Mexican divorce is probably shaky. You can definitely fight it when we get back."

Sommerhill swung around and faced him. "I don't want to *fight* it, man! The worst hangover I ever had was when I woke up *married* to that bitch! I just didn't know what to do, so I went along with it, figuring she wasn't bad lookin' and was good in bed. Hell, I've been gone so much anyway, I didn't have time to date! It seemed like it might work, until the fights started. Shit! She is a whacked-out druggie, crazy and meaner than hell! I'm glad she's gone . . . That ain't the problem."

McIver eased up toward the front seat. "I don't mean to break in here, but what is the problem, then?"

"She has all the bank accounts, charge cards, car . . . What about that shit? Can I stop that from going to her?"

"Oh, man." Neuhaus sighed. "Get Finance when we get back to Battalion. They'll stop the allotments from going to her. But if she divorced you—"

"She's spending the money!" Sommerhill interrupted. "She said in her letter that even though we're divorced now, she thought I'd be pleased to know she's donating *my* paycheck each month to the 'Divine Disciple's' account for help with their new enterprise, a television ministry out from Los Angeles!"

"Che-rist!" McIver hooted from the back. "She is nuts!"

"No shit!" he said, shaking his head. "She says we are brother and sister now, and since she still gets the money, she's putting it to good use."

"That can be stopped," Neuhaus said. "I'll get my old man to help . . . Send him the details when we get where we can transmit, and he'll get that shit stopped. It's not his field, but he knows how to do it, until you get back."

"Thanks." Sommerhill looked relieved. "She's already sold my Miata and bought a van."

McIver started to chuckle, aware that the emotions Sommerhill was feeling were not connected to any lost love, but his lost cash.

"Man, Eustas! She must be hell in bed. She's screwing the shit out of you right now, and she's ten thousand miles away!"

"Go ahead and laugh, Mac." He turned around angrily. "This could hurt my chances to make sergeant major!"

Stunned at Sommerhill's unprecedented statement of ambition, McIver sputtered.

"*Sergeant major!* Eustas, you're way out there now, what are you talking about?"

"If she gets my military ass in *debt,* is what I'm talking about! All I need is for the captain to start getting letters of indebtedness on me, and I can kiss my career good-bye!" He slumped in the seat.

McIver stared at him for a minute, then roared with laughter. "I knew it! I knew you were a lifer!" He reached up and leaned over Sommerhill's seat, trying to stop laughing. "Don't worry about this. It'll get ironed out. I think there's some sort of protection for soldiers in time of war . . . Isn't there, Neuhaus?"

"Yeah," Neuhaus nodded, "I think so. The Soldier and Sailors Relief Act covers some of this."

"See, Eustas!" McIver said, patting the man's shoulder. "You're gonna be all right. Hey," he said, "maybe it'll be deductible on your income tax . . . charitable donation to a religious institution!"

Neuhaus swung around and looked at McIver, shaking his head negatively. McIver cut his eyes, cautioning Neuhaus to remain silent.

Sommerhill's face lit up immediately. "You think so?" he said, cheerfully.

"Maybe . . . Now, let's talk about this 'sergeant major' thing . . . Are you serious?" Mac said, smiling broadly.

══ CHAPTER THIRTY ══

For four straight days and nights the bombers had dropped cluster bombs, detonating the mine fields on the Kuwait–Saudi Arabia border. Intelligence reports, garnered from Marine Recon units, Special Forces units in the area and aerial flyovers, all indicated that the 1st Armored Division, "Old Ironsides," could now move forward.

With M-60 mine plows running ahead of them, the great M1A1 Abrams tanks rumbled forward, Bradley fighting vehicles alongside, to meet the 2nd Armored Division of the Iraqi Republican Guard. The scene was a tanker's dream come true—hundreds of tanks and other tracked vehicles, escorted and flanked by thousands of infantrymen and weapons, with supply trains stretched out as far as the eye could see across the open plain. The air was full of Apaches, the flying tank killers.

The strong south winds could only hinder but never stop this advance. It was a scene that Cecil B. DeMille would have been proud of. But this wasn't Hollywood, this was reality. The defiant Iraqi Guardsmen were about to meet it.

Rolling with might and speed, the first unit to

approach the Saudi berm was Bravo Company. Line charges blew through the mine fields. The plows cleared lanes through the berms.

With lanes clear, Bravo's first platoon pressed forward. The four tanks of the platoon—"Devil's Daughter," commanded by Lieutenant George Petrie; Lieutenant Paul Sabler's "Christian Soldier"; "Bastard Boy," commanded by Lieutenant Dan Bigfoot; and Lieutenant Bob Fritz's "Hot Bitch II"—rumbled through the Iraqi mine fields.

Nearing the long-abandoned position first taken by Colonel Shadi's 2nd Iraqi Guard, Lieutenant Petrie hit the commo key. "Devil's Daughter calling Hot Bitch. Come in, Hot Bitch."

The receiver crackled. "Come in, Devil's Daughter. You have Hot Bitch here."

"Look at this. Appears they were here but gone," Petrie said as he looked over the deserted defenses. "Bastard Boy and Christian Soldier, are you reading this?"

"Bastard Boy is on your tail, Daughter. We read. Looks like the airboys took care of a couple of our playthings."

The sharp sound of an explosion echoed through the tanks.

"Hear all. This is Christian Soldier. M-60 and one Amtrak at four o'clock zeroed a mine. Christian Soldier unhurt and continuing."

Petrie thumbed the control. "Devil's Daughter here. Stay close, Christian Soldier." He chuckled as he turned to the loader sitting on the bench inside the dark cockpit. "Poor old Sabler," he said, referring to the commander of Christian Soldier, "he's in there just praying with all his might for us."

Lieutenant Sabler was a born-again Christian and had fought hard, but won no victory, to have the platoon name their tanks after the four apostles. He had a hard time calling the tanks by their crew-chosen names. In desperation he had named his tank "Christian Soldier." He was well liked and admired by the tankers, even though they hadn't changed the names of their tanks.

The "Hot Bitch II" was commanded by Lieutenant Bob Fritz, who'd named his tank after his Marine Corps brother's "Hot Bitch." The Marine Fritz was a warrant officer in the Reserves, who had now been called to active duty. Both Fritz brothers, one Marine and one Army, were tankers. Both were out today, hunting Iraqis in Kuwait, in their "Hot Bitches."

"Bastard Boy"'s commander was a native American, sub-chief of the Kiowa-Comanche at Ft. Sill when he wasn't busy tanking. Dan Bigfoot enjoyed his command, enjoyed the Armor, but longed for the end of his commitment, so he could return to Ft. Sill and assume his position as legal spokesman for his tribe.

The old defenses of the Iraqi Republican Guard were but a curiosity to the tank platoon. The trench offered no problem, and the treads of the mammoth machines left deep imprints over the remains of the ruined bunkers.

• • •

Shadi sent scouts forward several days earlier to report the coalition force's position. The scouts weren't back yet, and he was beginning to worry. The bombings had stopped around seven o'clock the night before.

This could be good or bad news, Shadi thought, as he rested on one of the carpets inside his bunker. It could mean that the war was advancing to the next stage, from the air to the ground. That would be good news. Or, he thought grimly, it's over and we've lost, without ever being able to face the Americans and their tanks.

As he stretched back on the rich carpet, he thought of how unfair it would be if that were true. How there would be no final conclusion, no final battle. The last order he'd received from Command Central was to fight. Now there was no communication at all, no Iraqi airplanes in the sky. The tanks were placed to defend, and defend is what Shadi intended to do.

He stood up and straightened his tunic. It was time to go outside and talk with the men. Their morale was low due to shortages in supply and lack of communication. As he walked out of his bunker toward the men, Shadi thought that perhaps he should have gone on the offensive, as Gallenz had done at Khafji. With the tanks he had had then, before the bombing, the outcome would have been different.

As he approached the troops at the edge of the ridge, he saw them pointing at two vehicles coming toward them across the desert. His scouts were

229

returning, moving much faster than he thought was necessary, given the short fuel supply. He stepped out in front of the men and waited as the jeeps geared down and came to a stop. The sergeant in charge jumped from the lead jeep and rushed up to him.

"Sir, they are coming. Many, many tanks have broken over the border. It is the American 1st Armored Division!" The man was breathless.

Shadi was elated; now the real battle would begin. "How far away are they?"

"Four hours at the most. They are headed directly toward us."

CHAPTER THIRTY-ONE

"There they are, Lieutenant! That's one of Vestal's," Jeep's driver said, as the dim outline of the TOW-mounted HMMWV came into view.

Walker hit the radio key and reported in to Battalion. "We have contact with Vestal's Virgins."

Each of Vestal's six vehicles appeared to be in good shape as the scouts rounded the dunes to meet up with the platoon commander in his lead HMMWV.

The storm was now nothing more than sporadic gusts of sand and wind. Laliker found Vestal, Hallmark and McIver repairing antennas.

Vestal stood and walked over as Laliker came to a stop and stepped out. "What brings you to our neighborhood?"

"Just out slumming. You really should police your area. You have old bodies and wrecks all over your backyard!" Laliker said, looking down at the antenna on the ground. "This your only casualty?"

Vestal nodded. "Yeah, we had some problems with the storm last night, too. I guess you know that, though."

"Rodwell wants an area recon. There's a lot of action south of us now."

Vestal picked up his canteen cup. "Just made some coffee. Join me?"

"Sounds good." Laliker turned to Walker. "Everybody out. Better get some food and rest for a half hour." Walker agreed and left to tell the others as Laliker and Vestal poured the coffee.

"I see you got those MK-19s up," Jeep said, pointing to the jerry-rigged mounts on the HMMWV. "Did you get to use them yesterday?"

"No, and they would have come in real handy. We got a break later and put them on. Thanks," Vestal said, stirring sugar into his coffee. "How'd the Rangers make out?"

Jeep gave a thumbs up, smiling. "Did good! Knocked the crap out of the command base and took prisoners."

"Prisoners?" Vestal wrinkled his brow. "I hadn't even thought of that."

"Yeah," Laliker said, laughing. "Seems the Iraqis have a lot of conscripts . . . and they don't want any part of this shitstorm Saddam stirred up."

They talked about the Ranger action and the fight the TOWs had had until Walker came back up, signaling an end to their break.

"Let's keep in close radio contact. What's your vehicle designation for commo purposes?" Laliker asked, standing to go.

"Old ABC system. I'll be in Alpha; my partner is Bravo; Charlie and Delta are the second pair of vehicles, and Echo and Foxtrot are the last pair."

Laliker noted the designations and turned to

leave. "We're Lima One, Two, Three and Four. I'm Lima One. Keep your head down!"

"You, too!" Vestal smiled as the scouts pulled away.

The American tanks reached the second mine field. The lead platoon fell back and assumed a watch as the engineers breached the field. Shadi's snipers fired on the mine sweepers from their protected positions.

The smoke, billowing from the flaming oil fields, provided the Iraqis with cover from the planes overhead, giving them time to set up their defense.

Colonel Shadi's plan was to use his T72s, the most mobile and powerful of his tanks, along with some BMPs, in a feint to the east. This he hoped would draw the American and allied forces into his densely bunkered positions. Here they would be vulnerable to the firepower of his less powerful tanks, which were dug in and waiting.

Besides the snipers, now busily harassing the mine sweepers from their locations on the ridge line, Shadi's infantry manned a series of trenches and bunkers defending the dug-in tanks.

Shadi gave the command for the T72s to move forward to a point out of range for the allied forces. His command vehicle remained concealed in a trench. The big Soviet-made tanks roared to life and clanked forward as the first of the allied tanks entered a lane now clear on the mine field.

• • •

Because of blowing sand and oil smoke, the Iraqis were not immediately identified, even with the thermal sights. Suddenly the driver of Devil's Daughter spotted the advancing T72s.

"There they are," he shouted, reaching for the commo switch. "Devil's Daughter has acquired contact with advancing enemy at four o'clock. Numerous T72s and BMPs. We are engaging."

Bastard Boy and Christian Soldier were next through the lane and flanked Devil's Daughter on both sides, turning their turrets toward the advance.

"Watch it! They're sucking you in," warned Fritz, as Hot Bitch II's driver pointed out the thermal images on the screen, showing the dug-in armor in Shadi's ambush. "Fire and hold till we get more of our boys up here."

"What's the range?" Petrie asked the gunner.

"Whoa! They're at thirty-seven hundred meters. It'll be tough to hit."

"Do it," Petrie said unhesitatingly.

The loader in Devil's Daughter quickly turned the sabot into the narrow circle and slammed the breech.

"Target tank at four o'clock," said the gunner as he squeezed the trigger on his yoke, causing the tank to leap back as the round thundered forward.

The round connected with the lead T72, sending sand and steel straight up, as the tank rocked from the hit.

The gunner in Devil's Daughter whistled. "Wow,

we waxed it!" It was the longest shot he'd ever fired.

The American gunner's surprise was nothing compared to the reaction of the Iraqi Guardsmen in the T72s. The advancing vehicles stopped and started to back away. Shadi, from his command tank in the trench, was stunned. Intelligence on the American tank had never reported its ability at a range over two thousand meters. Enraged, Shadi barked an order for the shaken T72s to advance.

More American tanks had struggled through the mine field and watched the Iraqi tank disintegrate. The lead enemy platoon was already in a position to engage them with frontal fire.

The Company commander was already on the radio.

"Don't let 'em get away. Continue to fire!" Disregarding the thermal images reported earlier, he sent the third platoon on line to the right, and the first on line to the left.

The dug-in Iraqi tanks began to fire on the nearing third platoon. Their first rounds, all short, inflicted no damage on the American tanks. Several of the Bradleys attacked the bunkers and moved forward, firing as they advanced. A swarm of Apache helicopters swooped in, firing Hellfire missiles into the tank positions.

The Iraqi infantrymen in the forward trenches sent out a heavy mortar barrage, then climbed out and engaged with the advancing allied infantry.

The four tanks of Bravo Company's 1st platoon

continued to fire on the advancing Iraqi T72s. Artillery now whistled past them, assisting in the attack.

Christian Soldier's gunner locked on a tank 2700 meters out and sent another sabot whistling across the sand. Inside the coffinlike turret, the spent round belched out of the breech. The loader stomped the floor pedal to the ammunition compartment and pulled out another round. The compartment closed, and he loaded the next round for firing.

"What's happening? Did we get it?" he asked the platoon commander, Lieutenant Sabler.

"Yes. Say a prayer for their souls!" Sabler answered.

The loader slammed the breech, muttering under his breath, "Fuck their souls!"

Two of the T72s pulled to a stop, their turrets turning. Bastard Boy had a round loaded, and the gunner trained his sights on the tank to the left.

"Target at two o'clock!" He flicked the yoke trigger, but the round never cleared the tube. The Iraqi T72's shell hit first. The Abrams rocked with the explosion, then burst into a fireball.

Watching in horror, the crew of Hot Bitch II swiveled their turret on the offending Iraqi tank.

"Eat this, you son of a bitch!" the gunner shouted, as he fired. The shell connected, exploding with a fury, as Christian Soldier eliminated the other tank. Proximity-fused-artillery rounds showered the now fully exposed infantry with fragments.

• • •

Shadi watched, stunned by the destruction being dealt his forces. His infantry, now scattered and in disarray, surrendered.

Crews from some of the tanks in the bunkers were climbing out, their hands high over their heads.

He grabbed the radio. "Retreat, all tanks, retreat!" The orders came too late for several more, as the American tanks and artillery continued to pound away at his position.

"Cease firing and hold your positions!" The American tankers stared at their radios in disbelief. The Iraqis were either surrendering or running away.

"What the hell?" Sabler said, to the surprise of his crew. He grabbed the radio. "This is Christian Soldier. Why are we stopping? Over."

"Battalion Orders, Christian Soldier. You, Hot Bitch, Devil's Daughter and Bastard Boy are to rotate to the back of the vee."

"Bastard Boy is hit." Sabler choked into the receiver.

There was a pause. "Sorry to hear that," the Company commander responded. "We are as far as we're going. The 3rd Armored Cavalry is moving on them now; they need some target practice. Those guys aren't going to make it to Baghdad."

Sabler looked out at the battlefield around him. There were smoldering wrecks in all directions. Bodies of Iraqi infantry lay scattered like old garbage across the sand. The survivors were already struggling toward the tanks, waving their hands high, over a hundred of them, trying to surrender. He focused his eyes on the still-burning wreckage of Bastard Boy. "Lord forgive me, but I hope they all rot in Hell!"

Tariq Shadi's vehicle led the retreat, pushing the surviving men and machinery at maximum speed into the oil-smoke cover of the burning fields, toward Iraq. He had no replacements, no reinforcements. The battle was lost. Now he had to regroup and survive to fight again.

The day had not been completely uneventful for Laliker and his scouts. They ran into a small platoon of Iraqi soldiers in a shelter near some rocks. The men were waving scraps of white paper over their heads as the scouts approached. Unsure of their intentions, the scouts fired a volley from the grenade launcher a hundred yards in front of the advancing soldiers, warning them to stop.

To Laliker and Walker's amazement, the men sat down on the sand and continued to wave the sheets of paper over their heads.

"What the hell is going on out there?" Laliker asked, as Walker opened the door of the HMMWV and started out toward them.

"Damned if I know. Cover me," he said, signaling for the HMMWV next to him to continue slowly behind him.

The first Iraqi to see Walker jumped up, crawled on his knees to him and embraced him around the legs. The man was sobbing, holding on to Walker.

The scouts in the other vehicles jumped out and pressed forward to join him.

Walker took the paper from the man's hand, looked at it and waved Laliker forward.

"It's terms of surrender. These are the pamphlets the air guys dropped. It's a guarantee of safe conduct. They've all got them."

"Let me see." Laliker looked down at the paper. It was done in English and Arabic with cartoon figures showing the Iraqis how to surrender to the allied troops.

"This is that slick stuff the Civil Affairs–PsyOps folks back at Bragg cooked up. Get on the radio and find out what we're supposed to do with them."

Walker freed himself from the Iraqi's grip and radioed back to Battalion.

In a few minutes he returned, shaking his head. "It seems everyone is taking prisoners. There are no available transports for them, so we have to take them to this point," he said, pulling out his map and tapping the spot. "It's an enemy POW pickup point."

"Pickup point? Sounds like something you do with laundry," Laliker said, glaring out over the twelve EPWs. Laliker put his hands on his hips and kicked at a clod of sand. "Send Williams and three others with Lima Four as escort. Damn," he sighed, wiping his forehead. "That leaves me a vehicle and four men short."

As Lima Four, escorting the EPWs, pulled away, the remaining three scout HMMWVs drove several kilometers southward toward the Kuwait-Iraq border. Walker spotted a rocky outcrop ahead, and the vehicles pulled over to set up camp for the night.

Battalion reported the 3rd ACR somewhere in the area, in pursuit of an escaping Iraqi tank company. The scouts were to continue the recon, but be aware of unfriendly activity in the region.

Smoke from the burning Kuwaiti oil fields drifted thickly over the horizon, at times obliterating all vision, as the scouts set up observation points on the road. They made camp, posted guards and then settled in for the night. Around dawn a heavy rain came pelting down.

== CHAPTER THIRTY-TWO ==

Laliker awakened to a rough nudge from Walker. He looked up at the man standing over him. "What?"

"Listen!" Walker said, kneeling down beside him.

Laliker could hear it, too, the faraway rumble and clank of tank treads. The sound came from the east.

"3rd ACR?" he said, looking up at Walker.

"Don't think so," Walker said, shaking his head. "They're a little more to the south."

Laliker sprang to his feet. "What do the lookouts see?" He grabbed his rifle.

"Nothing. There's heavy fog outside. That, mixed with the dust and oil smoke, makes it like looking at clam chowder."

As he spoke, one of the guards rushed over. He reported in breathless gasps that an enemy convoy of tanks and APCs was headed toward the road.

"Get Battalion on the horn," Laliker said, buckling his pistol belt. "How close are they?"

"They're too close!" was the excited reply.

Neuhaus responded immediately to the message, alerting Vestal. Pointing to the location on the map, Vestal ordered the TOW platoon into action.

As they sped down the road to set up defenses, the radio crackled again. Battalion informed them that the 3rd ACR was aware and within an hour of them. They were to set up defenses with the scouts at the highway intersection. Air support would be available as soon as the fog lifted.

"Lima One, this is Lima Three. We have been spotted by the enemy. I say again, we have been spotted."

A heavy round whistled overhead and exploded into the dune ahead of them before Laliker could respond. Large chunks of rock and earth, dislodged in the explosion, thundered down on the hood of the lead HMMWV. The vehicle stalled and stopped, slamming the men inside forward.

The driver tried to restart as another round slammed to ground to the right of them. There was only a grinding noise as the engine failed to spark.

"Out! Everyone get away from here! Scatter on the dunes!" Laliker yelled, grabbing a commo pack and yanking his driver from behind the wheel.

They rolled out onto the sand and scurried up over the dune. The third round from the Iraqi tank hit the crippled scout vehicle and sent it spiraling up in flames.

Walker grabbed the commo set from Laliker and yelled into the receiver. "Lima Two, this is Lima One. We're on the ground to the west of the turn in the road. We need pickup!"

"Lima One, we see you. Enemy infantry approaching on your right. Cover yourselves. We're on our way with a hot load."

The sound of the MK-19's slow popping followed by the sharp bangs of grenades filled the air. The screams of wounded and dying Iraqis proved the weapons' accuracy. Laliker and his men rolled into a tight tuck position down the side of the dune.

Walker skidded across the mud, joining Laliker and three other scouts.

"They're everywhere," he said, as a bullet zinged past him. Tracers flashed from the left, revealing a hastily set up Iraqi machine gun.

"Lima One, we've got a problem. Enemy BTR on my tail. Can't make the pickup. Lima Three on hard right of your position."

Laliker looked to his right and located Lima Three, racing down the road. He grabbed the handset. "Lima Two and Three, run for it! We're on the net!"

Machine-gun fire from the left had them pinned down. They concentrated their fire on the gunners and were trying to keep them down when a bullet thudded into the sand from behind them.

Walker rolled and returned fire, stopping the man running up on them. A deadly cross fire had them trapped now, as an Iraqi platoon swarmed the dune behind them.

Suddenly Lima Two rolled over the sand, blowing out the machine-gun nest with a volley from its M-19. The back door opened and two of the scouts dropped to the ground, firing at the Iraqi platoon with M-60s.

The Iraqi platoon dove back behind the dune for cover, firing sporadically at Laliker and the others as they ran for the HMMWV.

The scouts with the M-60s covered and jumped in last after the others had crowded into the already moving vehicle.

"Lima Three. Come in, Lima Three." Jeep waited for the response.

"Lima Three, go ahead."

"Lima Three, this is Lima Two. We've picked up passengers and are on our way to the road."

"We see friendlies on the intersection and are linking. There's a BTR behind me. Lima Three out."

Charlie and Delta TOW teams were first to spot Laliker's Lima Three headed toward them, closely followed by an Iraqi BTR. Charlie's gunner took aim and fired, tracking the enemy vehicle as the TOW's guidance wires sprang out like silken spiderwebs.

The BTR driver saw Charlie, too, but too late, as the missile slammed into the BTR and tossed the vehicle and its crew onto the side of the road. A secondary explosion ripped through the carrier, sending fire and debris into the early morning sky.

Delta team had targets as a Panhard and Cascavel topped the horizon. The gunner popped the Panhard first, then swiveled around, reloaded and hit the Cascavel. As he fired, the second pair of TOW HMMWVs, Alpha and Bravo, rolled into position, allowing Charlie and Delta to slide back and rearm their systems.

"Oh shit!" Neuhaus sputtered, pointing forward.

Five Iraqi tanks rumbled into sight, gun turrets lining up on the HMMWVs. Two BTRs pulled to a stop on the right side of the tanks, and their hatches flew open, unloading infantrymen.

Sommerhill lined up the array ahead of him. He exhaled and pulled the trigger. A thunderous boom rocked the HMMWV as his missile found its mark. He reloaded and fired again, then repeated the process until all six of his missiles were gone.

As the smoke and dust cleared, three of the tanks were on fire. Two others, crippled but not destroyed, swung their turrets wildly, firing harmlessly out into the distance. One of the BTRs lay on its side, its passengers scattered and crumpled on the sand. The enemy tankers lunged backward, searching for cover.

The other BTR had escaped untouched and unloaded. The squad of Iraqi infantryman quickly set up mortars and lobbed shells at the TOWs.

Bravo's gunner picked off the BTR, then swung back and put a round into the mortar positions.

The mortar rounds, already fired when Bravo's gunner blasted them, pounded the sand around Vestal's vehicles.

"Get us out of here," Vestal yelled at Neuhaus. The HMMWV lurched forward, then shot around to the side, falling back to reload. Echo and Foxtrot teams pulled up into firing position and waited for their targets.

Laliker, in Lima Two, lunged over the sand and zipped past the TOW teams toward the rear. Spotting Vestal and his crew loading the tubes on the TOW, he yanked on the driver's shoulder.

"Stop!"

Vestal turned as Laliker jumped from the scout vehicle. "Lima Three is over there," Vestal said pointing to the other HMMWV.

Laliker nodded, ordering his men out. "Cover the TOWs while they reload."

The scouts scattered over the area, guarding the TOW platoon from the encroaching enemy's sniper fire.

Reloaded, Vestal and his crew hurriedly took position. Echo Vehicle was on the radio.

"I think the Cavalry has arrived. The tanks have turned and are retreating to the left."

Vestal changed frequencies to Battalion Command and reported Echo's observations.

"Hold your positions. Do not pursue," the voice from Battalion responded. "Third ACR is moving in and will be on them shortly. Continue to block road. Scouts will go forward and report to you."

The fog was lifting. Broken rays of sun burned through the smoky haze. All firing around them ceased, as one of the scouts took out the last of the snipers.

The fighting had moved them back up on a small ridge line. Hallmark cautiously slid out across the sand to Vestal's vehicle and tapped on the side.

"I think we're clear for a while," he said, leaning against a wheel as the door opened.

Vestal dropped down on the ground next to him and watched as Hallmark lit his customary cigarette.

"Where're Laliker's other vehicles?" he asked, watching as the two scout HMMWVs pulled over the ridge.

"One is fried; the other took some EPWs back," Hallmark said flatly and took a deep drag.

"We went through some ammo back there. It'd be good to get a resupply."

"Neuhaus already called it in. Anybody hurt?"

"Charlie gunner caught some shrapnel. He's OK, but McIver will take his gun. Everything else looks good to go."

"What about the scouts, besides the HMMWV?"

"Laliker lost two men. Got chewed up by fire from a BTR."

Vestal moved his head from side to side, stretching the pinch in his shoulder muscles.

"Water," he said. "I need a drink. My mouth went dry an hour ago." He reached inside and pulled out his canteen. After a quick gulp, he handed it to Hallmark. "What are they doing? The Iraqis, I mean," he said, as Hallmark took a swallow and screwed on the cap.

"I figure they fell back, joined their main body and are about to shoot it out with the 3rd Cav."

═══ CHAPTER THIRTY-THREE ═══

Hastily prepared firing mounds hid the last of Shadi's remaining tanks. After his advance party's brush with the American missile unit up the road, his scouts had come in with reports of an advancing armored unit.

Bareem was standing before him now, pleading surrender. Shadi was tired, pushed and desperate. The last thing he needed was Bareem's whining. Several of his commanders huddled around, nodding as the pathetic executive officer pleaded his case.

"We're out of gas. We lost three tanks to the TOWs; several of our guns are disabled. The men are afraid to fire them." Bareem dropped his voice, continuing, "There's very little ammunition. We have no choice but to surrender."

Shadi's hand moved like lightning, yanking the pistol from his hip. He shot twice. Both bullets hit Bareem in the face. Shadi turned and pointed the gun at the onlookers.

"Cowards! We will *not* surrender. Get back to your men, or I'll kill you, too!"

His commanders stumbled backward, then recovered and hurried to their tanks. Any thoughts of surrender had now vanished.

Shadi slid into his personal T72M1 and stood in the darkness with his frightened crew. "We will fight! Those are our orders and I will see them obeyed! Load!"

Laliker and his scouts fought sporadic gun battles on the side of the ridge. Enemy troops had scattered out through the dunes and fired on the scout HMMWVs.

Walker leaned out the window, firing bursts as a small squad of Iraqis tried to block them. Laliker stood on the observation platform, firing out over to the left. They blew through the Iraqi squad, firing long bursts as the driver gunned the HMMWV and sped away.

Laliker slid down into the vehicle and reached over to tap Walker's shoulder. He stopped when he saw the blood. The driver was slumped over the wheel, holding his side. Walker was still draped out the window, his back turned to the inside. Bright crimson spots were spreading over the sandy camouflage pattern of his BDU tunic.

"Jesus! Bob!" Laliker grabbed the man and turned him around. Walker was dead. Before the realization could sink in, the driver moaned, causing Jeep to turn around.

One of the fallen Iraqis was back on his feet and hurling a grenade toward the HMMWV. Jeep saw it coming and yelled for the rest of the men to jump, pulling the driver with him.

The explosion caught them in midair, tossing the men across the sand as the HMMWV went up in smoke. Laliker hit the ground with a thud and rolled up, sending a burst from his M-16 into the Iraqi, who was preparing to throw another grenade.

As he fell, the grenade rolled a few inches from his hand and exploded, turning the sand a deep red with the remains of his body.

Laliker lay flat, struggling to regain his breath, then rolled over next to his driver. The man was in a fetal position, blood pouring from the wound in his side.

"Medic! Where is the medic!" Laliker yelled, as he ripped open the driver's shirt. It looked as if the bullet had entered above the hip and passed through beneath the rib cage. "Hang on," he said, patting the man on the leg. "You're going to be all right."

The medic low-crawled over and went to work on the man's wound.

"We need to get out of here, sir!" he said, as he popped a syringe of painkiller into the driver.

"No shit! Where's the radio?" Jeep asked the man behind him.

"Here, sir," one of the scouts answered.

"Get Battalion. Tell them we're falling back to the TOW position." He turned and looked up at the destroyed HMMWV. He could see Walker's body inside as the flames licked up around the vehicle.

Lima Three skidded to a stop, and several of the

men jumped out to help the medic lift the wounded driver inside.

A mortar round rattled overhead and hit behind the vehicle. The medic and wounded man were halfway into the HMMWV when the explosion rocked them. Fragments pelted the side of the vehicle as the other scouts dove for cover.

The medic grabbed the end of the stretcher and pulled the driver back out, throwing his body over him as the next mortar round hummed in. It exploded on the other side of the HMMWV, but fire from the explosion ignited the vehicle.

Two of the scouts rushed forward and helped the medic and the man on the stretcher toward the shelter of some rocks.

Another round screamed over Laliker's position, causing everyone to press into the sand. This round, though, came from behind them and ripped into the Iraqi mortar men.

Laliker looked up. It was Vestal. Corporal Sommerhill was sending a stream of 40-mm grenades into the Iraqis.

Vestal leaned out the window, yelling to them.

"Hold where you are! We're firing!"

Sommerhill squeezed the trigger and sent another burst arcing out, surprising an advancing Iraqi infantry platoon. The flurry of grenades blasted them.

Neuhaus revved the HMMWV forward to Laliker's scouts. They hurriedly loaded the wounded man and the rest of the scouts into the vehicle.

Two Iraqis stepped from behind the rocks and fired, pelting the HMMWV before Sommerhill saw them. He swung the gun over and fired the MK-19 into them.

"We gotta go, El-T!" he shouted, as the grenades did their work. The door slammed on the HMMWV, and they sped back to the waiting TOW vehicles.

"It's good to see you, but I thought you were supposed to hold your position," Laliker said, looking over at Vestal.

"Yeah, well it just seemed like the right thing to do at the time," he said, flashing a smile at Laliker. "Where's Walker?"

Laliker just shook his head.

"TOW Commander," the radio blared, "this is Hot Rod Twin, high in the sky to your right! Do you read me? Over."

Vestal held the handset and looked up. There were four Apaches streaking toward them.

"This is TOW Commander. I read you, Hot Rod. Over."

"Me and my boys are going to do a little cleanup work on your flank. Are all friendly folks forward? Over."

"Come on in, Hot Rod. No friends behind us. Over."

The Apaches whizzed past, blasting the landscape behind them with salvos of 2.75-inch rockets. Even the wounded man on the stretcher cheered.

Neuhaus pushed down on the gas pedal. The sting in his chest was worse. He'd felt a slam when

he Iraqis fired on them earlier. Now, as he rounded
he curve and pulled back between the other TOW
vehicles, he knew he'd been hit.

Vestal opened the door and jumped out to help
he scouts pull the stretcher out. Hallmark and
McIver joined them and pointed the way back to a
waiting Huey.

"Hey, Mike," Sommerhill said, climbing down
from his guns into the HMMWV, "we're bad . . .
Neuhaus?" He looked up at the driver's seat and
saw Neuhaus fall sideways.

"What's the matter with you, man?" As he leaned
forward, he saw the bullet holes in the door panel
first.

"Oh God! Medic! Get that medic back!" he yelled.

Neuhaus didn't need the medic.

Except for the smoke, the sky was clear. Helicop-
ers swarmed in over the horizon, leading the way
as the 2nd Squadron, 3rd Armored Cavalry Regiment, moved forward on the Republican Guard
positions.

As 1st platoon, C Troop, came forward, they took
fire from several Iraqi ZSU 23–4s and quickly
disposed of the enemy weapons. The Bradleys
soon came under direct small-arms fire. An RPG
round streaked just a few feet from a 1st-platoon
tank, and another passed by within six feet of a
Bradley.

"I've made their position and got a lock on them!"
shouted one of the Bradley's gunners, and he fired,

253

knocking out the trench-firing position of the Iraqi's.

The Republican Guard tanks began to fire. Within seconds most of 3rd ACR was engaged, firing volley after deadly volley into the weakened enemy positions. After ten minutes, they stopped.

Shadi knew, as the smoke cleared, that the battle was over. He had lost. Whatever was left of his Republican Guard was surrendering.

The crew inside his tank knew it, too. They turned to him, both begging him to surrender. Shadi knew he couldn't. He pulled his pistol and held it to the driver's head.

"Get us out of here! We're going back to Iraq!"

The frightened driver threw the tank in reverse, pulled away from the firing mound, then pushed the T72 into forward gear. He slammed his foot to the floorboard, making the tank grind up onto the road. They headed toward Iraq at maximum speed.

Confusion reigned on the battlefield as hundreds of Iraqis surrendered. The men of the 3rd ACR watched as they flooded toward them through the smoke and fire of burning tanks, hands high over their heads.

"Hey," one of the crew members on a Bradley said to his sergeant, "I thought I saw a tank moving back there."

The sergeant peered out through the thick, smoky air. "I can't see him. Which way was he headed?"

The soldier, not sure of what he'd seen, scratched his head. "North, I think."

"Not to worry, then," the tank commander responded. "He's headed straight into a TOW platoon from the 82nd. Get on the radio and tell them they're about to have company."

The Huey had just departed, carrying the wounded scout and Neuhaus's body away, when the transmission from the 3rd came in. Hallmark jumped behind the wheel of the HMMWV, yelling over his shoulder for Sommerhill. "Come on! I'm your driver now. Let's go get the bastard."

McIver and Vestal jumped into the other HMMWV. A hand shot out and grabbed the door just as they started off.

"One more passenger," Laliker said, yanking the door closed behind him. "I want to see how you guys do it."

Shadi's tank reloaded as he and his men sighted the TOWs in the distance.

"Fire!" he shouted to the nervous gunner. The round left the tube and whistled toward the HMMWVs. It smashed into the ground next to them, causing the vehicle to tilt forward, then roll over.

"Damn you!" Sommerhill yelled as he centered the target tank in his cross hairs. He thumbed the switch, sending his TOW into the T72.

The big tank exploded time and time again a the tank rounds inside it cooked off.

Hallmark reached up and tugged on Sommer hill's leg.

"Come on down, son," he said, looking from th burning rubble of the tank to the overturne HMMWV. "It's all over now."

CHAPTER THIRTY-FOUR

In Dhahran, Kobar Towers was full to capacity. The high rises were being used to house the various allied units as they awaited their flights back home.

Esprit de corps was the order of the day, as each unit proudly displayed their colors on the high rise they called home. Screaming Eagles, artistically painted on empty MRE crates, decorated the 101st Airborne's building. The 2nd Armored hung a banner the entire length of their tower, displaying their patch.

The 82nd was no exception; however, they added their own special touch with a jump tower on the roof. During the long days waiting for flights, the jump masters would gather there and call out jump commands, then hurl a dummy, complete with chocolate-chip fatigues, from the roof.

The other members of the 82nd would join in the fun, running to the balconies to repeat the jump master's commands. Even the spectators walking by would join in, as the Airborne strutted and played. A few units around them issued noise complaints, but no action was taken. Nothing could dampen the spirits of the soldiers. They knew they were going home wearing the laurel wreaths of victory.

Finally, the soldiers of D Company, 1/325th of the 82nd Division, stood in formation. Captain Rodwell mounted a platform to speak to them.

"Gentlemen, as you know, several members of this Company have been nominated for awards. We'll not be giving them out today, that ceremony will take place back home, but I'm proud to say we have one Silver Star and two Bronze Stars with V devices among the awards.

"You fought hard and well." Rodwell's voice grew thick as he continued. "I am proud to have had you all in my command. No man could ever go into battle with finer troops than you all are." He paused and looked out over them.

"We'll be returning home in three days. I'd like to announce a few people who've been promoted. Captain Lutell to Major, Lieutenant Jenkins to Captain, SFC. Bridges to Master Sergeant . . ."

"How long is this gonna take?" Sommerhill whispered to Hallmark, who stood in front, now leader of the platoon.

"Shut up, you're in formation," Hallmark whispered back, through clenched teeth.

". . . and Corporal Eustas Lee Sommerhill to Sergeant. Congratulations," Rodwell finished, scowling at Sommerhill. Snapping a salute to his men, he stepped down and told their commanders to dismiss them. Hallmark turned, unable to fight his smile as he looked into Sommerhill's surprised face.

"Dismissed!"

"Sarge, you should have told me." Eustas stared at the man, oblivious to the other members of the Company that walked by and patted him on the back.

"Eustas," Hallmark said, smiling, "have I ever told you how much I hate to be called 'Sarge'? The name is Van to my friends." He held out his hand. "Congratulations!"

Sommerhill shook his hand. "Thanks, Sar— Van."

Hallmark reached into his pocket and pulled out a set of new sergeant's stripes. "Here. These are yours. Let's go get them sewed on."

He took the stripes and looked at them, shaking his head.

"You know," he said, as they started back into their building, "I feel really good about this. I mean, I know I'm up for a Bronze Star, but the stripes mean more to me."

Hallmark stopped and looked at him. "What do you mean? You volunteered to go after those scouts. You and Neuhaus both did. That was some pretty heroic shit!"

Sommerhill smiled. "I just was there . . . you know. The stripes I worked for and feel like I earned. The medal . . . well, I was just at the right place, right time, doing my job. It's a freebie."

Hallmark grinned. "Let's get those stripes on and take you over to see someone who'll appreciate them."

The hospital in Dhahran was full to capacity, but, due to the lower-than-estimated casualties, it was filled mostly with doctors, nurses and corpsmen. The few patients received excellent care and abundant attention. This hospital was staffed by Reservists called to active duty for the war.

The large, open wards, each with ten to twelve beds, had long porches where the patients could go out and enjoy the fresh air.

Three of the patients from Ward B sat around a table with an umbrella, basking in the early morning sun.

"I've made a decision," Coy Vestal announced. "With all the money I've saved over here, I'm going to buy a new car." Vestal had a cast on one arm and bandages over the back half of his head.

Jeep Laliker, his cast-covered right leg resting on a stool, looked with surprise at him. "But what will you do with that old truck? You won't get rid of it?"

Vestal smiled. "That old truck has a history. It was my dad's. Some of my best memories are of times I used to sit on the ground and hand him tools while he worked on it. The day the Army came to tell us he was dead, I sneaked out of the house and hid. Didn't want anyone to see me cry. They found me there that night, sleeping on the front seat." Vestal paused. "No, I won't get rid of it, but I think I can have my own car now."

"Yeah," Jeep said, nodding. "You've decided what to buy?"

Coy straightened in his chair. "Do you think Corvettes are still hot with the women?"

"Yes, most definitely!" a slim, willowy brunette

nurse answered. She blushed, as the men all turned
toward her. "I'm sorry. I couldn't help overhear-
ing." She picked up her bandages and walked back
into the ward.

"Hmmm," Vestal commented, watching her walk
away. "I need to keep track of that one."

McIver stood unsteadily and reached for his
cane. "I'm due for X rays in ten minutes. They want
to check this new ball joint in my hip."

"Wait!"

They looked up and watched as Hallmark and
Sommerhill hurried down the porch toward them.

"Hi, sirs! Where you going, Mac?" Sommerhill
asked, handing McIver his cane.

"X ray. I'll be back in about thirty minutes. You
gonna stick around?"

"Let me escort you down there. After all," Eustas
tapped his new stripes, "we NCOs have to look out
for each other."

Hallmark, still chuckling as he watched him help
McIver away, pulled out a chair and sat down.

"So," he said, turning to Laliker and Vestal,
"what's the word? When are you guys going home?"

"We fly to Germany tomorrow and then on to the
States next week. What about you?"

Hallmark answered, "We will be standing on the
hallowed sands of Ft. Bragg in four days. That was
the word this morning."

Laliker leaned forward. "Is the 82nd going to
jump in, like you did when you came back from
Panama?"

"Shit no!" Hallmark said, laughing. "These guys

haven't made a jump in the entire time we've been over here. No way are we going to risk jump injuries, since we've come out of this so good."

Vestal and Laliker glanced at each other.

"Not everyone did so good," Laliker said, looking away across the beach. "I'm going to miss Bob Walker and my other scouts. We took a pounding before you guys pulled us out. Hell, Neuhaus died out there saving our butts."

The men sat in silence, remembering their lost comrades. "You know," Hallmark said quietly, "I learned something from Neuhaus. He and his family got crossed up, wasted a lot of time they could have had together. Now they've only got regrets. Ain't gonna happen to me. I'm gonna go back and remarry Gloria. We're going to make it this time."

Vestal reached over with his good arm and punched Hallmark's shoulder. "I think that's great, Van. When's the wedding?"

"Soon as you guys get back. I want it to be a family thing."

"We'll be there, won't we?" Vestal said, looking over as Laliker nodded. "We had a visit from Rodwell this morning," he went on. "Seems we're all going to be put in a new experimental unit. New weaponry, all new deal. Lieutenant Laliker here is going to join us."

"Sounds good. As long as we're still in the 82nd, I don't care," Hallmark said, standing. "I've got to go now, want to catch up with McIver and Sommerhill. Looks like you two have a visitor anyway. See you at Bragg."

Hallmark walked into the ward as Colleen Harrigan swaggered up to the table. "Well, see you guys survived your little accident in the HMMWV."

Vestal smiled and offered her a chair. "Jeep is just leaving. Have a seat."

"I'm not leaving. She came to see me. Have a seat, Colley. Say good-bye, Coy!" Laliker motioned to the seat next to him. "I have something I need to tell you, Colley."

"No! I have something to tell you both, I came to see you *both*." She continued to stand, her red hair glowing in the sun like copper.

They stared up at her.

"It's been fun . . . but we're going home now, and I'd like to remain friends with both of you."

"Friends?" Vestal said, looking at her in disbelief. "You and I are—"

"You and I?" she interrupted. "Hell, Laliker and I are the same. But I'm getting married when we get back."

"Married!" they both said, then looked at each other.

Vestal gulped. "Why, are you . . ."

"Pregnant?" She finished his question and laughed. "No, I'm going to marry my fiancé. I've been engaged for over a year now; it's time."

"Engaged!" Jeep sputtered. "I didn't know you were engaged."

"Hey," she said, turning to go. "You're both egotistical megalomaniacs, but not bad in bed . . . if you're not looking for anything more than physical

263

relief, that is. My man has more than that, and I'm going to go for it."

"What is he, a jet jockey?" Vestal asked.

Colley smiled and said proudly, "No, he's the manager of the new Kentucky Fried Chicken franchise at Ft. Bragg. Gotta go now. See you at home!"

They both sat there for a minute and then began to laugh. "Shit," Jeep said. "We've been beat out by a guy that fries chicken butts all day!"

Coy Vestal laughed again, this time almost falling from his chair. He regained his composure and looked around the porch. "Where *did* that nurse who likes Corvettes go?" He squinted again and reached up to smooth his hair. "Forget it! Look at that blonde walking down the porch."

Jeep looked over his shoulder. Maggie Cunningham waved, smiling as she walked toward them. "Get out of here, Coy. This is what I had to tell Colley. This one is mine."

Vestal hesitated, preparing to give Laliker a run for his money, until he saw the tears on Maggie's cheeks as she said Jeep's name. Vestal rose from his chair and walked into the ward. There would be no chance in that contest. Laliker was right; that one was his.

"The platoons will be strictly experimental," Rodwell said, looking across the desk at Vestal. "One will be commanded by Lieutenant Laliker and the other will be yours. Laliker's will perform scoutlike functions, but will do so with some rather fancy equipment. Your platoon will work primarily with the FOG-Ms, Fiber-Optic Guided Missiles. Any questions?"

"When do we start?"

Rodwell pulled a calendar from his drawer and flipped it open. "We'll assemble the men you'll need next week. The only person you have out on leave during that period is Master Sergeant Van Hallmark."

"That won't be a problem. Hallmark could lead anything. Staff Sergeant McIver will be the one to screen our people. He's hot on the FOG-M and knows what it will take to handle the system."

Wile Vestal talked, Rodwell nodded and wrote some notes on the calendar margins. "We'll be going up to the training grounds in Arkansas after that for a month to acquaint your people with their weapons and do some live firing," he said, looking over the rim of his glasses at the lieutenant across from him. "You healing up OK?"

"No problems, sir. I'm on limited PT right now, but I'll be ready to make the run next week."

"Good," Rodwell said, standing up and stretching. "Did I tell you that PFC. Neuhaus's father called here yesterday."

"Oh yeah?" Vestal said, cocking his head to one side. "What did he want?"

"Wanted to get in touch with Sergeant Eustas Sommerhill. Seems the last letter his son wrote them had just gotten in. Neuhaus asked his father to assist Sommerhill in getting his legal affairs straight."

"That's great," Vestal said, smiling. "I imagine that fancy New York law firm will never be the same after Eustas Sommerhill."

"There's more. Mr. Neuhaus put his son's car in storage when Mike joined the Army. The family wants Sommerhill to have it. How do you think he's going to look riding around in a black Bentley?"

Vestal's eyes widened. "Damn! Does he know about this?"

Rodwell shook his head. "No, I thought I'd let Mr. Neuhaus tell him. He's coming down here tomorrow, with the car, to consult with his client. The family also has some other things of Mike's they want to give Hallmark and McIver. I'm not sure, but I think its stocks and savings certificates. Evidently Mike had some pretty specific instructions in that letter. It's as if he knew what was going to happen."

"Yeah." Vestal looked down at his hands. "He was a good man."

266

"Speaking of 'good man,' aren't you supposed to be 'best man' in a couple of hours?"

Vestal looked up, smiling. "Yes, sir. You coming to the wedding?"

"Wouldn't miss it. See you there."

As he neared his new Corvette, Vestal saw a piece of paper jammed under the windshield wiper. "Shit!" he said aloud, yanking the paper out. "It can't be a ticket!"

As he read, he laughed. "Hey, butthead," the message stated, "If you can't catch a woman with this vehicle, maybe you better think about the priesthood. See you at the wedding. Jeep."

"Eustas, I'm gonna tell you one more time, then I'm gonna knock the shit out of you if you ask me again! I *know* what I'm doing. I'm marrying Gloria . . . again. Only this time, we've got it right!" Hallmark calmly reached over and flicked some lint off Sommerhill's uniform. He smiled broadly. "I'm a happy man today. I've got all my family together—Gloria, the boys and you guys. It couldn't be better."

Rays of sunlight flickered through the stained-glass window of the chaplain's office and cast brilliant colors across the room. Van Hallmark, attired in his dress blues, straightened his own rows of ribbons and glanced down at his watch. "Just go out there, make sure the place is set up right, get the folks seated and stop worrying about me."

Sommerhill nodded, started for the door, then

turned. "OK, Van. I'm just checking. You're always so busy takin' care of my business, I just wanted to—"

"I know," Hallmark interrupted, laughing, "you're just being a good NCO, taking care of your troops."

Sommerhill beamed. "Yep, I guess that's part of it. Good luck, Sarge!" He turned and walked out the door. As he left, Coy Vestal entered through the chapel door.

"I just got a look at your bride, Van. I'm not sure you're good enough for her. I might just have to marry her myself," Vestal said as he walked over to Hallmark, still using his cane.

Hallmark smiled. "She looks good, huh?"

"Sure does. This is a fancy wedding for the second time around."

"Yeah, well, Gloria always wanted us to get married in a church. The first time we did this it was in front of a justice of the peace at Ft. Benning. I figured we'd do it her way this time, start out in front of God and everybody. You got the rings?"

Vestal feigned surprise, patting all his pockets. "Rings?"

"Don't clown around, sir," Hallmark said, frowning.

"I've got them right here." Vestal opened his right hand to display the two golden bands. "Don't start getting nervous on me, Van. We've got forty-five minutes to go before the ceremony starts. I don't think I can handle having you get shaky."

Hallmark sat down on the couch and motioned

or Vestal to have a seat in the chair across from
iim. "You're right. Let's just visit here for a while."

Still standing, Vestal pulled a silver flask from
iis inside pocket. "Thought I'd bring you some
Dutch courage.' Are there any glasses in here?"

"On the shelf behind you."

Vestal nodded, selected two, then walked over to
he chair by Hallmark. He split the contents of the
lask into the glasses, handed one to Hallmark,
hen sat down. Holding his glass up, he said, "To
/our happiness."

Hallmark smiled, touched his glass to Vestal's,
ind they each took a sip.

"Thanks, El-T," Hallmark said, as the warm
;low of the Tennessee whiskey hit him. "I needed
his."

"I saw Captain Rodwell this morning. Talked to
iim about the new platoon we're forming. We're
;oing to do some training next month in Arkansas.
They have some new weapons for us to try out."

"Yeah." Hallmark leaned back on the couch and
iut his feet on the coffee table. "I heard already.
Gloria and I plan on getting away for a couple of
veeks after the reception. Figure we'll take the
ioys to Disney World down at Orlando. I told her
ibout the Arkansas trip, and she seems OK on it.
Ve figure we got to make the most of the time we
iave together, 'cause we'll spend a lot of time
ipart, at least until I retire."

"Good," Vestal said, running his finger over the
im of his glass. "I'm glad to hear that. It was your
raveling that busted you two up before, wasn't it?"

Hallmark shook his head. "No, at least not entirely. I think we forgot what was important. We know now, and we can make the compromise. I'm looking forward to getting back to work. Seems like all we've done since we got back from the sand is go to parades and memorial services."

"I meant to thank you for going up to Neuhaus's service. I couldn't get them to release me from the damned hospital in time. How did it go?"

"Sad." Hallmark stood and walked to the window. "Just a family that shares too many regrets now, instead of good memories." He turned and faced Vestal. "Not like Bob Walker's service. All his brothers and sisters were there, lots of kids everywhere. They were sad to have lost him, of course, but they couldn't stop telling stories of how they each remembered Bob, how much fun they had together. The Walkers are a very close family. Even the brother that runs the fishing business is a great guy, but I could see why Bob couldn't work for him. They were too much alike."

"Did you see Laliker there?" Vestal asked, setting his glass on the table.

"Yeah, and that good-looking woman he found in Saudi, too. What's her name . . . ?"

Vestal smiled. "Maggie Cunningham. She is something, isn't she? Think ol' Jeep got real lucky there. She left the day before we did and met our plane when we landed. I don't think they've been apart since we got back. She leaves next week though, for Texas. Has to get one last semester in at college."

"Then what?" Hallmark asked, already knowing [t]he answer.

"I imagine I'll be pulling duty as 'best man' [a]gain, around Christmastime. Jeep couldn't find a [b]etter deal."

The door opened and Harold McIver entered. [']What is this?" he asked, looking at the glasses on [t]he table. "You two in here boozing it up in the [c]haplain's office?"

Hallmark held up his empty glass. "Yeah, and [t]he El-T, being an officer and a *gentleman,* only [b]rought enough for one drink!"

McIver pulled a sack from behind his back.

"That's why," he said, with a rakish grin, "God [g]ave NCOs imagination. Here's just a wee bit of [S]cotch to wet our whistles." He pulled out a bottle [o]f Johnny Walker Red. "Now, if you'd show me the [g]lasses . . ."

Vestal got up and grabbed another glass as [M]cIver and Hallmark settled on the couch. "Here," [h]e said, handing the glass to Mac. "How's it look [o]ut there?" he asked, motioning toward the chapel [a]s McIver filled the glasses.

"People are just starting to come in. The parking [l]ot is already crowded, though. Gloria is in the [b]ride's room already. Her mom and dad are in [t]here with her." Mac screwed the top back on the [b]ottle as Van and Vestal picked up their drinks.

"I have a toast," McIver said, holding his glass [h]igh.

"It's a day for them. Go ahead, Mac." Vestal stood [a]nd held his glass up.

"I wrote this on the way over; you'll have to giv
me a minute . . ." Mac pulled a piece of pape
from his pocket. "Ah, yes, here it is . . ." He hel
his glass high. "I have ridden the skies in grea
machines, hooked up and jumped with the best
men. I have fought long and hard, and when I fe
I had no energy left, I have been fired by the fea
that if I stopped fighting, my comrades would di
And when I was in danger, enemy all around,
heard the thunder from my left and my right, a
my life was defended. I have never been alone.
live, jump, fight and battle to victory with th
greatest assemblage of men on earth. Gentleme
to the brotherhood of the Airborne."

As their glasses clinked together, each man mu
mured, "To the Airborne!"